When the Nines Roll Over

ALSO BY DAVID BENIOFF

The 25th Hour

WHEN THE NINES ROLL OVER

(and Other Stories)

DAVID BENIOFF

VIKING

VIKING
Published by the Penguin Group
Penguin Group (USA) Inc., 375 Hudson Street, New York, New York 10014, U.S.A.
Penguin Books Ltd, 80 Strand, London WC2R ORL, England
Penguin Books Australia Ltd, 250 Camberwell Road, Camberwell, Victoria 3124, Australia
Penguin Books Canada Ltd, 10 Alcorn Avenue, Toronto, Ontario, Canada M4V 3B2
Penguin Books India (P) Ltd, 11 Community Centre, Panchsheel Park, New Delhi - 110 017, India
Penguin Group (NZ), Cnr Airborne and Rosedale Roads, Albany, Auckland 1310, New Zealand
Penguin Books (South Africa) (Pty) Ltd, 24 Sturdee Avenue, Rosebank, Johannesburg 2196, South
  Africa

Penguin Books Ltd, Registered Offices: 80 Strand, London WC2R ORL, England

First published in 2004 by Viking Penguin, a member of Penguin Group (USA) Inc.

10 9 8 7 6 5 4 3 2 1

Copyright © David Benioff, 2004
All rights reserved

"When the Nines Roll Over," "The Devil Comes to Orekhovo" (as "The Affairs of Each Beast"),
and "Neversink" first appeared in *Zoetrope*; "Zoanthropy" in *Tin House*; and "De Composition" in
Faultline.

PUBLISHER'S NOTE
These selections are works of fiction. Names, characters, places, and incidents either are the product
of the author's imagination or are used fictitiously, and any resemblance to actual persons, living or
dead, business establishments, events, or locales is entirely coincidental.

LIBRARY OF CONGRESS CATALOGING-IN-PUBLICATION DATA

Benioff, David.
    When the nines roll over, and other stories / David Benioff.
        p. cm.
    ISBN 0-670-03339-1
    I. Title.
    PS3552.E54425W47 2004
    813'.6—dc22   2004049613

This book is printed on acid-free paper.

Printed in the United States of America

Designed by Carla Bolte   Set in Aldus with Aperto display

For Amanda—
I love you.

CONTENTS

When the Nines Roll Over

WHEN THE NINES ROLL OVER

SadJoe is a punk rocker, he rents by the week
and if his landlord ups the rent he'll be living on the streets
he's never had a run of luck, deuces load his deck
his rottweiler's name is Candy and she's tattooed on his neck
his girlfriend sells tickets at the Knitting Fac-to-ry
she gets him in to see the bands and every band for free
so raise a glass for SadJoe, for SadJoe raise a glass
he's going, going, going gone but going with a blast!

The singer had presence. She wasn't a beauty, and her pitch was imperfect, but she had presence. Tabachnik watched her. Lord, the girl could yell. From time to time he surveyed the young faces in the crowd. The way the kids stared at her—the ones in back jumping up and down to get a better look—confirmed his instinct. The girl was a piggy bank waiting to be busted open.

Tabachnik and a foul-smelling Australian stood by the side of the stage, in front of a door marked REDRÜM STAFF ONLY!

Most of the kids in Redrüm were there to see the headliners, Postfunk Jemimah, but the opening act, the Taints, was threatening to steal the show. There was no slam-dancing or crowd-surfing or stage-diving—everybody bobbed their heads in time with the drummer's beat and watched the singer. She prowled the stage in a bottle-green metallic mesh minidress so short that Tabachnik kept dipping his knees and tilting his head to see if he could spot her underwear. He could not spot her underwear.

When the band finished the song Tabachnik turned to the Australian and asked, "What's that one called?"

The Australian had recently started an independent label called Loving Cup Records. The Taints were the first band he signed. His head was shaved and his black tracksuit stank of sweat and cigarette smoke.

"It's good, huh? 'Ballad of SadJoe.' SadJoe's the drummer. He started the band."

"Who writes the songs?"

"Molly," said the Australian, pointing at the lead singer. "Molly Minx."

She didn't look like a Molly Minx. Tabachnik wasn't sure what a Molly Minx should look like, but not this. He guessed that she was Thai. Her hair was cropped close to the scalp and bleached blond. A tattooed black dragon curled around her wrist.

"The story is," continued the Australian, "she has a big crush on SadJoe, and she writes this song, and one night she sings it to him. Right on the street, a serenade. So, you know, love. Boom. And he asks her to join the band."

Tabachnik had never heard of the Australian before tonight, which meant that the Australian did not matter in the music business. Whatever contract Loving Cup Records had with the band would be a mess, whipped up one night by a cocaine-addled lawyer who passed the bar on his third try. That was Tabachnik's guess, anyway, and he was generally right in these matters.

Making money off musicians was so easy that third-rate swindlers from all over the world thought they could do it; they swarmed around talentless bands like fat housewives around slot machines, drinking cheap beer and exchanging rumors of huge payoffs. Third-rate swindlers were doomed to serve as rubes for second-rate swindlers—unless they were unlucky enough to get conned by a true pro.

After the Taints finished their set Tabachnik retreated to the VIP room with the Australian. He expected the man to light a joint and offer him a hit; when it happened Tabachnik shook his head and took another sip of mineral water.

"I got you," said the Australian, leaning back in the overstuffed sofa. He sucked on the joint and kept the smoke in his lungs for so long that it seemed as if he had forgotten about the exhale part. Finally he released the smoke through his nostrils, two plumes curling toward the ceiling. It was an impressive gesture and Tabachnik appreciated it—Australians were always doing shit like this—but it was meaningless. He wasn't going to deal with Loving Cup unless it was necessary, and at this point he doubted it would be.

"I got you," repeated the Australian. "You want to keep a cool head for the negotiations."

"What negotiations?"

The Australian smiled craftily, inspecting the ash at the tip of his joint. He had told Tabachnik his name. Tabachnik never forgot names, but in his mind the Australian was simply "the Australian." He was sure that he was simply "major label" in the Australian's mind, but eventually he would be "that fuck Tabachnik."

"Okay," said the Australian. "Let's just talk then."

"What should we talk about?"

"Come on, come on. Let's quit the gaming. You're here for the band."

"I don't understand something. You've signed Postfunk Jemimah?"

The Australian squinted through the haze of smoke. "The Taints."

"So what are we talking about? I'm here for Postfunk Jemimah."

"You like the Taints," the Australian said, wagging his finger as if Tabachnik were a naughty child. "I saw you checking on the crowd. Well, you want them?"

"Who?"

"The Taints."

Tabachnik smiled his version of a smile: lips together, left cheek creased with a crescent-shaped dimple. "We're having a conversation here, but we're not communicating. I came to see Postfunk Jemimah."

"Too late, man. They signed a six plus one with Sphere."

"Right," said Tabachnik, rattling the ice cubes in his glass. "And we're buying Sphere."

The Australian opened his mouth, closed it, opened it

again. "You're buying Sphere? I just saw Greenberg two nights ago at VelVet. He didn't say a word."

"Who's Greenberg?"

The Australian laughed. "The president of Sphere."

"Green*spon*. And he's required by law to keep silent about it. I'm breaking the law telling you, but"—Tabachnik indicated the empty room with his free hand—"I know I can trust you."

The Australian nodded solemnly and took another deep hit. Tabachnik figured he would need forty-eight hours to get the girl. The last thing he wanted was for this pissant label to sniff out his interest and put the chains on her, rework her contracts. If that happened he would have to buy out Loving Cup, and Tabachnik hated paying off middlemen. In the grand scheme of things, the musicians made the music and the consumers bought the music, and anybody in the middle, including Tabachnik, was a middleman. But Tabachnik did not believe in the grand scheme of things. There were little schemes and there were big schemes but there was no grand scheme.

"I can introduce you to Heaney," said the Australian, desperate for an angle. "He manages Postfunk Jemimah."

"Yeah, we went out for dinner last night. But thanks." Tabachnik gave another tight-lipped smile. All of his smiles were tight-lipped because Tabachnik had worn braces until a few months ago. He wore the braces for two years because his teeth had gotten so crooked that he would bloody the insides of his lips and cheeks every time he chewed dinner. The teeth were straight now, the braces gone, but he had trained himself to smile and laugh with a closed mouth.

He was supposed to get braces when he was twelve, like a normal American, but his mother and father, who had split up the year before, kept bitching about who ought to pay for it. "Your only son is going to look like an English bookie," his mother would say into the telephone, smoking a cigarette and waving at Tabachnik when she saw that he was listening. "Excuse me, *excuse* me, I *would* have a job except you know why I don't? You know who's been raising our son for the last twelve years?"

So when the money for the orthodontia finally came, Tabachnik told his mother he didn't want it. "Sweetheart," she said, "you want to be a snaggletooth all your life?"

Tabachnik found the negotiations over his teeth so humiliating that he refused to have them fixed. He never again wanted to depend on another man's money. He worked his way through college in New Hampshire, copying and filing in the Alumni Office, until he figured out better ways to get paid. He convinced the owner of the local Chinese restaurant to let him begin a delivery service in exchange for twenty percent of the proceeds; he hired other students to work for tips and free dinners and to distribute menus around town. Tabachnik made out well until the restaurant owner realized he no longer needed Tabachnik. That incident impressed Tabachnik with the importance of a good contract.

He managed a band called the Johns, a group of local kids who worked as custodians and security guards at the college. The Johns always sold out when they played the town bars, and Tabachnik took them to a Battle of the Bands in Burlington, Vermont, where they came in second to a group called Young Törless. Young Törless became Beating the

Johns and had a hit single remaking an old Zombies song. Tabachnik was reading *Variety* by this point, and he saw how much money Beating the Johns made for their label, and he thought, Jesus, they're not even good. And he realized that good doesn't matter, and once you realize that, the world is yours.

When Postfunk Jemimah began to play, Tabachnik and the Australian went to listen, and afterward joined them, their manager Heaney, and the Taints for a postgig smoke session in the club owner's private room. The VVIP room. Tabachnik had been places with four progressively-more-exclusive areas, where the herds were thinned at each door by goons with clipboards, turning away the lame. Some of these rooms were so hard to get into that a full night would pass without anyone gaining entrance. People who had never been turned away before, people unused to rejection, seven-foot-tall basketball players and lingerie models with bosomy attitude, would snipe at the bouncer and declare their lifelong friendship with the owner, and the bouncer would nod and say, No. Tabachnik wasn't a VVVVIP, but he didn't care. He suspected that if you ever got into the fourth room you would find another closed door, leading to an even smaller room with even fewer people, and if you could somehow convince the bouncer to let you pass, you would enter a still-smaller room, on and on, until finally you would find yourself in a room so cramped only you could fit inside, and the last bouncer, the biggest, meanest one of all, would grin at you before slamming the pine door and lowering you into the ground.

Tabachnik asked Heaney to speak with him in the other

room for a minute; they huddled in a corner of the single-V VIP room and ignored the wannabes who stared at them and wondered who they were.

"Congratulations," said Tabachnik. "I hear you signed with Sphere."

"Yeah, they own us forever, but we're good with it."

"I need to ask you a favor . . ."

When they returned to the VVIP room, the Australian stared at them unhappily. Heaney gathered his band and they went off, in high spirits, to eat pierogi at Kiev. Tabachnik stayed, as did the Taints and the Australian, who slouched with the discontent of the small-time.

"Well," said the Australian, passing a joint to SadJoe, "next year in Budokan."

There were no chairs or sofas in the room, only giant pink pillows. Everyone sprawled in a loose circle and Tabachnik felt like an adult crashing a slumber party. Only Molly Minx sat with her back straight, very erect and proper. Her legs were propped up on a pillow and Tabachnik studied them: they were tapered like chicken drumsticks, thick with muscle at the thighs, slender at the ankles. She wore anklets strung with violet beads and black slippers like the ones Bruce Lee wore in his movies. Her hands were clasped together in the taut lap of her green dress; her face was broad and serene below her bleached, spiked hair. Thai or Filipino? She smiled at Tabachnik and he smiled back, thinking that a good photographer could make her look beautiful.

The guitarist began to snore. The bassist was crafting little soldiers from paper matches; he had a pile of Redrüm matchbooks beside him and he arrayed his army on the gray carpeting. They were very well made, with miniature spears and a general on a matchbook horse, and Tabachnik watched, wondering when the war would begin.

SadJoe was shirtless. His black mohawk was spotted with large flakes of dandruff. A rottweiler's head was crudely tattooed on his neck, the name *Candy* inked in green script below the dog's spiked collar. The air was rich with marijuana smoke and body odor. SadJoe puffed on the joint contentedly until Molly elbowed him.

"It's a communal thing, lover."

He grunted and passed her the joint; she smoked and passed it to Tabachnik; Tabachnik took a hit, let the smoke sit in his mouth for a moment, and breathed out. He passed the joint to the bassist and asked the drummer, "How'd you get the name SadJoe?"

SadJoe made a gun with his thumb and index finger and shoved it into his mouth.

Molly said, "He's sick of telling the story."

If you're going to call yourself SadJoe, thought Tabachnik, you ought to expect a little curiosity.

"I'll tell it," said the Australian. The whites of his eyes were now mostly red. A strand of mucus was creeping out of one of his nostrils and Tabachnik started to say something but then decided not to.

"SadJoe grew up in New Jersey," the Australian began. "What town?"

"Near Elizabeth," said SadJoe.

"Near Elizabeth. And the street he lived on, I guess this

was a quiet town, all the kiddies played together. Football and so forth."

"Street hockey," said SadJoe. "Street hockey was the big game. I was always goalie. Goalie's the best athlete on the team." He nudged Molly Minx and she smiled at him.

"So they all played street hockey together. This was before SadJoe became SadJoe. He was just Joe."

"Some people called me Joey."

"All right. And along comes a new family, with a little boy. This boy, unfortunately, was born a little off. Special, you call it?"

"He was a mongoloid," said SadJoe. Molly shot him a nasty look and SadJoe shrugged. "What's the nice word for mongoloid?"

Everyone looked at Tabachnik. There was something about his face that made people suspect he knew things that nobody else would bother to know.

He said, "A kid with Down's syndrome, I guess."

"Mon-go-loid," said SadJoe, chanting the syllables into Molly's ear. "Mon-go-loid."

"But a sweet boy," continued the Australian. "Always smiling, always laughing."

"He used to kiss me on the lips sometimes," said SadJoe, scratching his armpit. "But I don't think he was gay. Sometimes retards don't know the difference between right and wrong."

"Jesus," said Molly.

"Well," said the Australian, "the boy's name was Joe. But the kids couldn't call him Joe, because our friend here already had the name. So they started calling him Happy Joe."

"He was a good kid," said SadJoe.

"And eventually," concluded the Australian, "if there's one Joe called Happy Joe, then the other will become Sad Joe."

"Ta-da," said Molly, lighting a new joint.

"And they all lived happily ever after," said the Australian, gazing hungrily at the fresh weed.

"Not really," said SadJoe. "Happy Joe got run over by a UPS truck."

Everybody stared at him. He sighed and rubbed the palm of his hand over the stiff ridge of his mohawk. "First dead body I ever saw."

"You never told me that part," said Molly, frowning.

"Death makes me glum, baby."

The club closed down at four in the morning, but Tabachnik and the Taints stayed until five, when the manager came to say they were locking the doors. They shuffled outside and shivered on the street corner.

"You know what we should do," said SadJoe. "The fish market opens up in a few minutes, down on Fulton Street. We should go down there."

"Why?" asked Molly. She was wearing an old fur coat. One of the sleeves was torn, but it looked like real fur.

"That's when the fish is freshest," SadJoe explained.

The Australian and the bassist and the guitarist murmured stoned good-byes, hailed a cab, and headed for Brooklyn. Finally, thought Tabachnik.

"If you two want to grab some coffee, there are things I'd like to talk about."

"Nah, I guess I'll go home," said SadJoe. "First train will be running pretty soon."

Molly stared at Tabachnik and then at SadJoe. "Maybe we should get some coffee."

"Not for me, pretty. It's fish or nothing." He extended a hand for Tabachnik and they shook. The drummer had a firm grip. "Later, pilgrim."

"Why don't you invite him to the party," said Molly, still staring at SadJoe purposefully.

SadJoe looked at her, raised his eyebrows, and then shrugged. "I'm having a party tomorrow afternoon. In Jersey."

"We can go together," Molly told Tabachnik. "His place is hard to find."

Tabachnik gave her a card from the hotel where he was staying, his room number already written on top in neat, square digits. "Give me a call. I'd love to go."

SadJoe watched this exchange in silence, chewing his lip. Finally he said, "Tell me your name again, man."

"Tabachnik."

"Yeah, all right. We'll see you."

SadJoe and Molly Minx walked away and Tabachnik watched them go, SadJoe's heavy black boots clomping on the pavement, the back of his old army jacket scrawled with faded words in black Magic Marker.

· · ·

The next afternoon Tabachnik picked up Molly at the occult boutique in the East Village where she worked. They took the subway to Penn Station. Tabachnik had not ridden the subway in years. He longed to be back in Los Angeles, where there were supposedly millions of people but you never really saw them. He could walk two miles in his neighbor-hood, on broad sidewalks beneath tall palm trees, and en-counter one old woman in yellow pants and one small boy on a skateboard. Everybody else was locked away some-where safe.

Tabachnik and Molly Minx held on to a metal pole as the train shuddered and plunged through the tunnel. He wore black woolen pants, a black cashmere turtleneck sweater, and a full-length black peacoat. Molly wore a powder blue catsuit that zipped in the back. Winter wasn't over yet, and this is what she wore. She had what seemed to be a perma-nent wedgie. All the men within sight had noticed this con-dition. An old man chewing a potato knish stared at her ass, glanced at Tabachnik, and then resumed staring at her ass. The other men pretended not to stare at her ass, pretended to look up only at appropriate moments—as when the con-ductor announced something unintelligible—and then sneakily stared at her ass. When Tabachnik caught them they would quickly look away, but Tabachnik *wanted* people staring at her ass. He wanted the whole world horny for Molly Minx.

They boarded the 4:12 from Penn Station and sat in the back car. Tabachnik paged through four different music magazines he'd bought that morning. Molly played games on her cell phone.

When the train shot out from under the Hudson, the pale New Jersey sunlight seemed strange and hostile. They sped through industrial flatlands, past smokestacks that pointed to the sky like the fingers of a giant hand. As the train began to slow down Molly said, "This is us," and Tabachnik thought she was joking. People didn't live here.

They walked past sprawling chemical plants ringed with chain-link fences topped with concertina wire. Warning signs were posted every few yards. Do Not Enter and This Area Strictly Off Limits and No Trespassing. Everything stank of methane.

SadJoe's street was normal and suburban—two parallel rows of ranch houses with aluminum sidings—except that it was the only residential block in the entire industrial complex. In front of each house was a tidy lawn. Leashed dogs growled. Tabachnik and Molly walked below the outflung branches of leafless red maples.

SadJoe's house was the last in the row. There was a barbecue party in the backyard. SadJoe stood at the grill, a bottle of beer in one hand, a pair of tongs in the other. He wore black sweatpants and no shirt, though the temperature was in the forties. Tabachnik noticed, for the first time, that SadJoe's chest and arms were crosshatched with fine, pale scars. Candy, the rottweiler, sat by her master's feet. When SadJoe flung her bits of charred beef, the dog would snatch them out of the air and lick her black lips.

Tabachnik followed Molly to the grill, watched her kiss SadJoe on the mouth, watched the drummer's bottle-holding hand slide over her ass. When they disengaged, SadJoe nodded to Tabachnik, gesturing with his tongs and beer bottle to indicate that he could not shake hands.

"Well," said SadJoe, watching the hamburgers sizzle above the coals, "welcome to the neighborhood."

There was a long silence until Tabachnik pointed at the scars on SadJoe's chest and asked, "What are those?"

"Huh?" SadJoe bent his head and studied his own skin. "Oh. Razor scars."

Tabachnik waited for the rest. When he realized it wasn't coming, he asked, "Why do you have razor scars on your chest?"

"From when I was in high school. How do you want your burger?"

Tabachnik shook his head and explained that he had eaten earlier. A keg of beer sat in a red plastic tub of ice. A picnic table with a black-and-white checkerboard tablecloth held bowls of potato salad and coleslaw, bottles of cola, and a chocolate cake with the number "200,000!" in yellow icing. Most of the men wore work boots, blue jeans, and plaid flannel shirts. They stood in small circles drinking beer from Dixie cups and yelling at SadJoe to quit burning the goddamn burgers. SadJoe would give them the finger each time and the men would laugh and resume their conversations. The women sat at the picnic table. They watched Tabachnik and Molly and spoke in low tones.

An older man, his eyes bright blue beneath savage strokes of white eyebrow, sat with the women. He wore a Jets football jersey with NAMATH embossed on the back on top of the number 12. When he saw Molly he stood up and limped over to her. He kissed her on the cheek.

"This is SadJoe's father," she told Tabachnik. "We call him OldJoe."

"Not around me, you don't."

OldJoe grinned and shook Tabachnik's hand. His grip was as firm as his son's. "Help yourself to some beer, friend. I'm going to check on Joey's mom."

He limped to the house, opened the screen door, and disappeared inside. The sky began to darken. Somebody turned on the floodlights and people ate their burgers and drank beer and cola and Tabachnik wondered if he was the only one about to die of exposure. It was the first week of March. Who had outdoor barbecues the first week of March?

After dinner everyone gathered on the front lawn. SadJoe and his father and several of SadJoe's friends were inside the garage. An engine revved and the crowd on the lawn cheered.

Molly smiled. "He's been looking forward to this for three years."

A black Ford Galaxie 500 rolled out of the garage, glistening in the floodlights with a fresh coat of wax. Everyone but Tabachnik whooped with pleasure. SadJoe sat in the driver's seat, his black mohawk brushing against the car's roof. His father sat beside him. Four other men were crammed into the backseat. All the windows were down and the car's speakers were blasting a song Tabachnik recognized. "The Ballad of SadJoe."

SadJoe waved his friends over to his window and one by one they came. Each leaned into the cabin, looked at something on the dashboard, and then shook SadJoe's hand. When it was Molly's turn she leaned in and kissed her boyfriend for a long time, and people started whistling and making smooch-smooch sounds. When she stood up she beckoned for Tabachnik. Tabachnik did not want to lean into the cabin and he guessed that SadJoe didn't want him to either. But Molly kept curling her finger and everyone seemed to be waiting, wondering who he was, so Tabachnik went to the side of the car and crouched down until his head was level with SadJoe's.

SadJoe pointed at the odometer. "What does it say, pilgrim?"

Tabachnik squinted at the numbers, white on a black field. "Ninety-nine thousand nine hundred and ninety-nine."

"And nine-tenths. I've already flipped the first hundred. This is mile number two hundred thousand coming up."

"Wow," said Tabachnik. *Wow* sounded ridiculous, but what was he supposed to say?

He shook hands with SadJoe and backed away. SadJoe pulled himself halfway out of the window and called out to his assembled friends: "Everybody who's helped with this car over the years, Gary and Sammy and Gino, thank you. Thank you, Lisa, for the hubcaps. Molly, thanks for my song. Mom, if you can hear me in there, thanks for never complaining when I practiced the drums. And most of all I want to thank dad for buying me this car when I was in high school, when it only had ninety thousand miles on it."

Everybody clapped and whistled and SadJoe put the Galaxie into gear and rolled into the street. He took a left and drove very slowly and all his friends walked behind him. Candy, loyal squire, trotted alongside the car. Tabachnik followed in the rear. He glanced at SadJoe's house and saw an old woman standing in the window, the curtain pulled back and gathered in her hand. She was watching the car's stately progress. She looked much older than SadJoe's father.

In the middle of the block SadJoe hit the brakes, leaned on the horn, and began yelling and pumping his left fist out the window. The four men in the back jumped out and high-fived each other as if the Jets had finally won another Super Bowl. The crowd cheered and started singing "The Ballad of SadJoe" a cappella. A few boys about high school age set off a round of fireworks. Everyone watched the rockets hurtle into the dark sky above the brightly lit street, higher and higher and higher, disappearing into the blackness, everyone still watching, their faces upturned to the nighttime sky, waiting for the rockets to burst, for petals of blue flame to drift slowly downward. Everyone watched for a full minute, until it became certain that the rockets were duds.

· · ·

On the train ride back to Manhattan, Tabachnik asked Molly if she loved SadJoe. It wasn't a question that he had planned on asking, and he didn't think it was a smart question to ask, but he wanted to know.

She was staring out the window. She said, "I guess there was a Shell station near where he grew up. And him and his friends, they had a rifle, and every now and then they'd get drunk and shoot out the *S*. You know, make it the 'hell' station. And the next week there'd be a new *S* up there and Sad-Joe and his friends would go over and shoot it out again. They got caught, finally. And the judge said, well, this is the first time you've been in trouble, and he let SadJoe go. His friends had records, so they were sent to a JD center. Anyway, a week later he shot out the *S* again. And they brought him back to the judge and SadJoe said, 'I want to be with my friends.' "

Tabachnik nodded and studied the various New Jersey towns listed on the train ticket. He did not believe the story. It was too romantic, too perfect a history for a rebellious punk rocker. But he thought about the street SadJoe grew up on, with its concertina wire and methane stink, and he thought about the razor scars, and the mother behind the window with the curtain bunched in her hand, and he thought about the friends who had piled into the backseat so they could be there for mile number two hundred thousand, and he thought if anyone would shoot the *S* out of the Shell station sign so he could join his buddies in the JD, it was SadJoe.

Tabachnik did not want to say any of this to Molly, so instead he said, "Hell is other people."

Molly turned away from the window and stared at him. "Really?"

"No, I mean, that's a quotation. I didn't make it up."

She rested her head on his shoulder and said, "I never heard that before."

Tabachnik stared out the window but it was too dark to see anything outside. He saw his own face reflected in the glass, and Molly's bowed head, and the empty seats around them.

· · ·

They went to a twenty-four-hour Turkish restaurant on Houston, drank small cups of bitter black coffee, ate syrupy baklava. The Turk manning the cash register had the *Daily*

News crossword puzzle on the counter between his elbows. He chewed on the eraser-end of a pencil.

"I'm going to make you a star," Tabachnik told Molly. He never smiled when he said these words; he never made a joke of it. He said the line very simply, enunciating each syllable, looking directly into the listener's eyes. He knew that every kid in America was waiting to hear those words, or at least all the kids who mattered to him. They wanted to believe him. They needed to believe him.

Molly took a deep breath. She smiled and looked down at her fingers picking apart the layered pastry. She looked very young, very shy, a blushing girl on her first date.

"I'm going to fuck you anyway," she said. "You don't have to blow smoke up my ass."

Tabachnik made eye contact with the Turk at the counter. The Turk grinned.

"Check," said Tabachnik.

• • •

She had a small room in an Alphabet City apartment that she shared with five other musicians and actors. She led him by hand through the shadowy hallways, guiding him past piles of dirty laundry, a sleeping dog, and a bong lying on its side in a puddle of bong water.

When they got to her room she closed the door and slid a dead bolt shut. She saw Tabachnik's raised eyebrows and said, "Weird things go on here. A guy got knifed on New Year's Eve."

Tabachnik didn't want to know about it. He held the side of her face and kissed her on the lips and she unbuckled his belt and unzipped his pants and he thought, Jesus, what's the rush? And then he realized that he was very, very old. Soon he would have no idea what kids wanted to hear on the radio. A&R men did not age gracefully—you either moved up or were bumped off. Tabachnik was good, a rainmaker for all seasons, but he had never had the huge score. He had never signed a group that became a super group, a Nirvana or R.E.M or Pearl Jam. The men who signed the super groups were no longer A&R. They were VVVVIPs.

He unzipped the back of her catsuit. Her skin was beautiful, the color of a cinnamon stick, and it flushed in the places where his mouth went. She shimmied out of the suit and stood naked before him, her hands covering her crotch with mock bashfulness. Tabachnik kissed her throat and her breasts and her belly, crouching lower and lower until he was on his knees.

When they finished they lay on their backs in bed and listened to the sleeping dog in the hallway moan in his dreams.

"I want to fly you out to L.A. and have you record a few demos."

"We have demos," said Molly, pointing to a black boom box piled with cassette tapes.

"I want them done right. We can fly out tomorrow."

"What about everyone else? I'm not just going to leave them."

Yes, you are, Tabachnik wanted to say, but instead he traced circles around her nipple with his fingertip and said, "I don't have the money to fly the whole band. We'll get you out there, have you meet a few people, send for everyone else later."

"SadJoe won't like it. The Taints are his band."

"I'll tell you what, Molly, the Taints might be his band, but you're the one people want to see. You're the one writing the songs. I was watching the kids at the club the other night, I was watching who *they* were watching, and it was all you. Nobody cares about the drummer."

"I care about the drummer."

Tabachnik had worked in this business for ten years and he'd come to believe that loyalty only existed when it was convenient for all parties. He'd never seen a band that he couldn't break up. He took no pleasure in splitting these people apart, he wasn't a sadist, but he felt no guilt either. They all believed they were destined to be stars and they were very sad to leave their friends behind but they got over it quickly. They understood that not everybody could be a star.

Tabachnik looked at Molly Minx and saw that she was looking at him. She was waiting to hear the rest. She would argue with him, but not with much passion.

"You're the one with the talent," he told her. "I like SadJoe, he's a good kid, but you're the one with the talent."

"I don't even know what talent means," she said. She waited for him to speak but he kept his silence; he wanted her to give it a little effort. She wrote a song for the poor kid, she could at least give him a mild defense.

"I don't think I *believe* in talent," she said at last.

Tabachnik believed in talent. A band he was scouting had opened for Buddy Guy in Atlanta and Tabachnik had stayed for the main act, had listened to Buddy Guy play guitar. On the drive back to his hotel, Tabachnik had thought, *I'll never be that good at anything.* It wasn't a big deal—most people would never be as good at anything as Buddy Guy was on the guitar. It was sad to realize you were lumped with most people, but it wasn't a big deal.

Still, he understood what Molly Minx was talking about. He wasn't trying to sign her because of her talent; she saw through that bullshit. He wanted her because she would sell records. That didn't mean she was talented and it didn't mean she was talentless. Talent was irrelevant to the equation.

"Listen," he told her, "I'm putting you in a difficult position, I understand that. But it's not that complicated. Come with me to L.A. and good things will happen for you."

She stared up at the batik tapestry that was tacked to the ceiling and didn't say anything.

"Oh," he added, "do you have a copy of your recording contract lying around?"

"I think so. Why?"

"Let me take a look at it."

She got out of bed and he sat up against the headboard and watched her squat beside a blue milk crate and rummage through a manila folder filled with receipts, bills, and certificates. He liked the efficient lines of her body. She looked like she could squat for hours, a peasant shelling peas.

When she found the contract he took it from her and studied it carefully. It had been printed on a dot-matrix printer with a dying ribbon. One page. A brown stain from a coffee mug neatly ringed the signatures. Tabachnik sighed.

People were so stupid he no longer took pleasure in their stupidity.

"What's your real name, Molly?"

"Jennifer." She was sitting on the edge of the bed, watching him.

"Your whole name."

"Jennifer Serenity Prajadhikop."

"Where are you from?"

"Toronto."

"Really? Okay. Serenity. That's good. We'll need to retire Molly Minx."

He folded the contract and handed it back to her. She fanned herself with it and said, "I can do that. I was getting kind of sick of it anyway. I've been Molly Minx since high school."

· · ·

The next day he took her out for lunch and then to the label's New York office. The receptionist sat behind a horseshoe-shaped desk sheathed in black granite. Behind her, twenty-foot-high windows stared out at the Hudson River.

"Good afternoon, Mr. Tabachnik. Good afternoon, Serenity."

Molly squinted at the woman as if trying to place her from high school days, and then she said, "Hey!" and tugged on Tabachnik's jacket sleeve. "They already know me!"

He took her into an empty conference room, left her staring at the platinum records on the wall and the giant photographs of smirking singers. In an unused office he phoned Steinhardt, the label's president, and waited for the assistant to patch him through.

"Tabachnik? How's our girl?"

"We got her. Schmucks had the group signed to a two plus one, but they have her listed in contract *and* in signature on her stage name."

"Ha, I love it. Well, they might sue on breach of good faith."

"I already faxed a copy to Lefschaum. We're clear."

"Yeah, good faith my left nut. Get her out here. Get her name on a six plus one and let's make this girl happen."

"It turns out she's Canadian."

"Uh-huh," said Steinhardt. "Everyone turns out to be Canadian."

Tabachnik didn't know what that meant. When you were the boss, you got to say inscrutable things and everybody would nod as if Confucius were just reborn and not a minute too soon.

"How's the wife?"

"Lenis?" asked Steinhardt, as if the word *wife* were too vague. "She's in Montana this weekend with the dogs. I better run, buddy. Listen, good job. You're my ace."

Tabachnik hung up the phone and stared out at the Hudson. A Circle Line boat was pushing north through the gray water. Tourists pressed against the starboard railing and snapped photographs of the Manhattan skyline. Tabachnik waved. Their flashbulbs flashed, pointlessly, and Tabachnik waved both hands, knowing he would never show up in any of the pictures.

. . .

Nothing went wrong. He flew back to L.A. with Molly Minx. She began introducing herself as Serenity—"Just Serenity," she told people—but he still thought of her as

Molly Minx. He had one of the girls from the label take her shopping on Melrose, and that night she modeled her new outfits for him. He told her she looked good in vinyl and she said, "Are my breasts too small?"

He thought they probably were but he shook his head and said, "Not for me."

They decided that she would stay in his apartment for a few weeks, until she learned her way around the city. He wasn't used to having a roommate. He hated sharing breakfast, hated having to say "Pass the orange juice, please," hated to hear about her ornately symbolic dreams from the night before. But Tabachnik noticed that the apartment felt empty when she was away. He noticed that he was almost always happy to hear her key turning the lock. They would put her face on television soon, they would put her face on CD sleeves and promotional posters and billboards, but right now he was the only one looking.

She signed a contract rendering exclusive recording services to the label for six records, plus a seventh at the label's option. When she received her advance she held the check between both palms as if fearing that the zeros might roll off like stray Cheerios. That night she took Tabachnik out for sushi on Ocean Avenue and forced him to drink shot after shot of sake with her. He got drunk for the first time in years. Later, at home, he knelt before the toilet, returning fishes to the sea, while she sat on the edge of the bathtub, writing lyrics in a spiral-bound notebook.

The next morning he was in a nasty mood. He left the apartment without waking her and went straight to work.

His assistant was already there. She greeted him cheerfully and Tabachnik smiled his tight-lipped smile and closed the office door behind him.

He skimmed the trades, glancing at each headline and noting names and dollar amounts. He paged through poorly written reports from junior A&R reps and then jotted a few comments on Post-its that he stuck to the appropriate demo tapes stacked on his desk: *pretty boys + good dancers; lead sing hot black chick; lead sing Marc Bolan's son.* He checked his e-mail quickly, deleting messages marked URGENT! from agents and managers, scanning a tedious missive from Steinhardt, deleting a long list of dead lawyer jokes sent from the London office, opening a file attachment and staring at a photograph of his baby nephew. He could see no family resemblance, which he figured was lucky for the kid, and he deleted the file.

The last message came from Joseph Paul Bielski. Tabachnik had not heard the name before. He opened it and read: THIS IS TABACHDIK HE GOT SHOT IN THE HEAD •:(THIS IS TABACHDIK AND THERES A SPEER STICKING IN HIS HEAD--->:(THIS IS TABACHDIK HE GOT SHOT IN THE HEAD BUT HES OKAY ABOUT IT •:) AND THESE ARE THE SPREAD CHEEKS OF MY ASS)*(SAYING KISS ME TABACHDIK! SEE YOU SOON, SADJOE.

He called for his assistant and when she came into the office he pointed to his computer screen and asked, "How did this guy get my e-mail address?"

She read the message and laughed. "Tabachdik? What is he, five years old?"

"I don't give this out to strangers. Did somebody call here asking for it?"

She closed her eyes and rapped her forehead with her knuckles. "Thinking, thinking . . . yes! Somebody called."

Tabachnik stared at his assistant and wished that he were a woman, a very large woman, so he could pound the little twit senseless.

"Look, I've told you before, take a message and I'll contact them. Okay? Assume that everyone calling is a psychotic. All right, good-bye. And no more, okay? Next you'll be giving these fuckers my home address."

His assistant had the door halfway opened. She stopped and looked back at him, her mouth open in a small *o*. "Ooh," she said. "Uh-oh."

· · ·

Tabachnik asked Molly if SadJoe still had the rifle he used to shoot out the *S*'s. She didn't know. He asked her if SadJoe was the sort of person who might plot a violent revenge. She pursed her lips, thought about it for a while, and said, "No."

Tabachnik wasn't satisfied with that answer. If the kid cut *himself* with razor blades, what would he do to the man who stole his girlfriend and broke up his band? So Tabachnik shacked up with Molly in the Chateau Marmont for a week. He showed her the room where John Belushi overdosed and the lounge where the guitarist Slash fucked his girlfriend on a glass-topped table until the glass shattered and both of them had to be rushed to the emergency room.

They had drinks on the flagstone patio—Jack and ginger for her, mineral water for him—and she said, "And this is the patio where SadJoe murdered Tabachnik."

This struck her as extremely funny and she laughed and laughed. Her hair was now fire-engine red.

When the week was over Tabachnik decided he would not be intimidated by a New Jersey punk who lived with his parents and had dandruff in his mohawk. He and Molly returned to the apartment in Santa Monica. He had a deadbolt installed on the front door. He took his name off of the building's intercom box. He borrowed a pit bull from an agent who was going to Cannes for two weeks but the dog refused to eat his food and cried all night and Tabachnik finally had the agent's assistant retrieve it.

He waited and waited and finally it happened. Tabachnik and Molly were lying in bed, smoking and watching an old episode of *The Jeffersons*. It was just after one in the morning. All the lights were out in the apartment. Tabachnik wasn't holding Molly's hand but their shoulders and hips were touching. By this time, of course, she could afford her own place, but he kept forgetting to tell her that.

George Jefferson launched one of his tantrums—eyes wide with shock at the world's injustices—and was interrupted by a loud drum roll. Tabachnik frowned. The drum roll wasn't part of the show. The drum roll wasn't coming from the television. He looked at Molly and Molly closed her eyes and smiled.

They listened. SadJoe was playing from the sidewalk. He was loud. He was pounding on the skins, and the quiet street echoed with the sound. *Bud-a-bum-bum-BOM-bud-a-bum-bum-BOM-bud-a-bum-bum-BOM-BOM-BOM-bud-a-bum-bum-BOM.* It wasn't music, it was violence with a rhythm.

Tabachnik wondered if the kid was good. It was hard to tell. Who listened to punk-rock drum solos? He found himself tapping the bedspread nervously with his palms, keeping time, and he stared at his hands as if they were traitors.

"That fucker," said Molly, laughing. "That little fucker."

SadJoe played so hard the windowpanes rattled. He played so hard he silenced George Jefferson. He played so hard every dog on the block began to howl, howling with the last traces of wolf blood remaining in their plump domestic bodies.

Tabachnik lit a new cigarette. "I guess it's a serenade."

Molly covered her face with a pillow and Tabachnik wondered why. Was she laughing back there? Crying? People were already beginning to yell at SadJoe. Shut up! they yelled. Hey! Asshole! Shut up! Hey!

Tabachnik got out of bed and opened the curtains. He opened the glass sliding door and stepped out onto the narrow balcony that overlooked the sidewalk. Up and down the street people were standing on their balconies or leaning out their windows to watch. SadJoe sat behind his kit in the middle of the sidewalk, ignoring the catcalls, pummeling the drums and toms. The bare scalp on either side of his mohawk shone in the streetlight. He was shirtless, and the muscles of his shoulders and forearms coiled and uncoiled beneath pale skin.

Tabachnik sucked on his cigarette and rested his elbows on the concrete parapet. The Galaxie 500 was parked in front of a fire hydrant. SadJoe's army jacket rested on its roof. Two Golden Arches—three-foot-high yellow McDonald's Ms—leaned against the black car's rear bumper.

SadJoe looked up and saw Tabachnik standing on the balcony. He jumped off his stool and pointed toward his enemy with a drumstick. "FUCK YOU, TABACHNIK! FUCK YOU!"

Tabachnik tapped off his ash and sighed. SadJoe was the good guy in this situation. There was almost no way of reckoning the past events and coming to any other conclusion.

"WHERE'S MOLLY? MOLLY! MOLLY!"

Tabachnik turned and looked into the bedroom. "He's calling for you."

Molly pulled the pillow off her face and sat up in bed. "Jesus, Joe. What are you doing to me?"

Tabachnik stared at the burning tip of his cigarette for a long while before looking down at SadJoe again. "She wants you to go away."

"FUCK YOU, TABACHNIK!"

Directly below Tabachnik the building's front door burst open and a big man in a white T-shirt, plaid boxer shorts, and black basketball shoes charged toward SadJoe and his drums. SadJoe saw him coming and said, "This isn't about you, pilgrim."

Tabachnik recognized the man as one of his downstairs neighbors. A stuntman—no, not an actual stuntman, a stunt coordinator. Something to do with stunts. He had explained it one time. Tabachnik would run into him and his girlfriend at the mailboxes and they would all exchange pleasantries, and one time the man spoke about his profession, how he arranged for cars to vault fallen bridges or roll down steep embankments. He had always been friendly but it seemed that he hated to be awakened by drum solos.

SadJoe said, "Hold on, brother," but the stuntman wasn't listening. He dodged around the kit, grabbed SadJoe in a headlock and started punching the drummer's face. Whack. Whack. Whack.

Tabachnik puffed on his cigarette and watched. The stuntman threw SadJoe into the drums and the kit toppled to the pavement, boom stands clattering on the concrete, brass cymbals ringing as they rolled back and forth on their rims.

Tabachnik winced. He turned and said to Molly, "He's getting his ass kicked."

She jumped out of bed and made for the balcony, fists clenched at her side.

"You're naked," said Tabachnik.

Molly stopped in midstride and looked down at her naked self. She seemed surprised, as if she had never seen her breasts before, her belly.

She crossed her arms over her chest and stared sadly at Tabachnik. "He needs me."

Tabachnik stubbed out the cigarette on the parapet and walked back into the bedroom, pulled on a pair of pants and a sweatshirt.

"Where are you going?" she asked.

"I'm going out there before he gets his neck broken."

"Why?"

Tabachnik shrugged. It was complicated. He left the apartment, jogged down the stairs, pushed through the building's front door, and hurried over to the fight. Except the fight was over. SadJoe was lying on the sidewalk, bleeding from the nose and mouth. The stuntman was smashing the kit, putting his shoe through the kick drum, slamming a floor tom against the pavement, breaking the stands over his knees.

"Hey!" yelled Tabachnik. "Enough!"

The stuntman glanced at Tabachnik and then walked over to the Galaxie 500, the broken end of a cymbal stand in his hand. He started swinging at the yellow McDonald's Ms.

Tabachnik, barefooted, stepped around the shards of broken drum equipment and grabbed the stuntman's arm. "Enough," he said.

The stuntman wheeled around and punched him in the nose. Tabachnik went down. He surprised himself by quickly standing up. He even swung at the stuntman. It seemed like the thing to do. He swung as hard as he could, got his whole body into it, hit the stuntman flush on the cheek. The stuntman frowned and punched Tabachnik again, and this time there was no getting up.

Tabachnik sat slumped against the fire hydrant. The stuntman surveyed the damage for a moment and then went back into the building, stomping on a snare drum for good measure.

The curbside was littered with yellow plastic splinters. The golden arches lay facedown on the street, their backsides burnished aluminum. Tabachnik heard police sirens in the distance. He looked over and saw SadJoe crawling through the wreckage of his kit.

"Are you all right?"

"Fuck you, Tabachnik."

"That's the first fight I've been in since fifth grade."

SadJoe wiped his nose with the back of his hand and stared at the blood. "You call that a fight?"

"I got one punch in."

SadJoe sat cross-legged with the kick drum on his lap. He ran his fingers over the perforated skin. Blood leaked from his nostrils, ran in rivulets over his chest, seeped into the waistband of his camouflage pants. He tilted his head back and stared skyward. "This kit cost me two thousand dollars."

"I'll get you another one."

"Hey, fuck you, man. Fuck your money."

People were still watching from their windows. A young man standing on a balcony across the street, wearing tightie-whities and a Dodgers cap, recorded the scene with his video camera. Tabachnik checked his teeth with the tip of his tongue. They were all there.

"I want to talk to Molly," said SadJoe, his head still held back, the kick drum in his lap. "I want to give her the Ms."

"The thing is, it's over. She doesn't want to talk to you."

SadJoe snorted loudly and spat a gob of blood and phlegm onto the pavement. He looked very tired, sitting beneath the flickering streetlight. Of course he looks tired, thought Tabachnik. His girlfriend abandoned him, his best shot at stardom was destroyed, he drove cross-country to win back his girl and got beat up by a stuntman. A stunt coordinator.

"She didn't need you," said SadJoe. "She could have been a star in New York, she could have been a star in Toronto. She was going to be a star no matter what. The cream will rise to the top."

"No," said Tabachnik. "It won't." Whatever was floating on top, it wasn't cream.

"She didn't need you," SadJoe repeated, slapping the side of the broken drum. "It was my band but she was the star and that was cool. I don't give a fuck if you don't believe me. I just wanted to sit back there and lay down the beat and watch her. You're going to put her with some studio guy who sounds like a fucking drum machine. Why, man? I'm not greedy. I just want to make a living, it doesn't have to be fancy. So why? I'm not good enough? Is that it? You think I'm not good enough?"

"I don't know," said Tabachnik. It was the most honest answer he could give. "I don't know anything about drumming. You sound fine to me."

"So why?"

"It had nothing to do with you."

SadJoe laughed. "Jesus, Tabachnik. Don't you have any imagination, man? Don't you have any fucking imagination? You think you turn the corner and I disappear?"

Tabachnik stared up through the palm fronds. The moon was nearly full and the clouds frothed like boiling milk. Closer to earth, Molly Minx stepped out onto the balcony and leaned over the parapet. She had put on an oversize hockey jersey. The red bristles of her hair looked like tiny flames rising from her scalp.

SadJoe saw her and scrambled to his feet. "Molly!" he yelled. And again, more quietly, "Molly." He pointed to the broken Golden Arches. "I brought you a couple Ms, but that big guy busted them."

"It doesn't matter," she said. "My name is Serenity now."

"Okay." He nodded and rubbed his forearm under his nose. "Serenity's a good name."

"You need to go home, Joe. You can't keep stalking me."

"Stalking you? I'm not stalking." He looked at Tabachnik for support. Tabachnik shrugged.

"Go home, Joe." She walked back into the apartment and slid the glass door shut.

SadJoe stared up at the empty balcony for a long time. Finally he turned to Tabachnik and lifted his shoulders in a gesture of surrender.

"Next year in Budokan," he said. He grabbed his army jacket, got into the Galaxie 500, and drove away, leaving behind the ruined drum kit and shattered Ms. Tabachnik watched the car's taillights until they were out of sight. His nose did not hurt very much and he figured the stuntman had pulled his punches. In a few minutes he would stand up and walk back into the building, climb the stairs to the second floor, return to his apartment, and lie down again with Serenity. But not yet. He wanted to sit for a moment and think.

All the street's balconies were empty now, the windows dark again. The show was over. He wondered how far SadJoe would drive, where he would pull over for the night. Nobody could drive straight through from Los Angeles to New Jersey, but Tabachnik couldn't imagine SadJoe stopping at a motel to sleep. He could only picture the drummer driving, his hands on the steering wheel keeping the beat of the radio's song. Driving past mountains and deserts and strip malls and farm fields, never stopping, never stopping, alone in his black Galaxie, the odometer ticking off each tenth of a mile.

THE DEVIL COMES TO OREKHOVO

The dogs had gone feral. They roamed the countryside in packs, their claws grown long, their fur thick and unbrushed and tangled with thistles. When the soldiers began marching at dawn, Leksi counted each dog he spotted, a game to help the time pass. He quit after forty. They were everywhere: crouched and watchful in the snow; racing through the shadows of the towering pines; following the soldiers, sniffing their boot prints, hoping for scraps.

The dogs unnerved Leksi. From time to time he would turn, point at the closest ones, and whisper, "*Stay.*" They would stare up at him, unblinking. There was something strangely undomestic about their eyes. These dogs lacked the wheedling complicity of their tamed brothers; they were free of the household commandments: *Do not shit in the kitchen. Do not bite people.* A silver-haired bitch still wore a purple collar, and Leksi imagined that the other dogs mocked her for this badge of servility.

Of the three soldiers, Leksi, at eighteen, was the youngest. They marched in single file with ten-meter intervals between men, Leksi in the rear, Nikolai in the middle, Surk-hov in front. They wore their gray-and-white winter fatigues, parkas draped over their bulky packs to keep everything dry in case of snowfall. We look like old hunchbacks, thought Leksi. His rifle strap kept slipping off his shoulder so he ended up holding the gun in his gloved hands. He still wasn't used to the rifle. It never seemed heavy when he picked it up in the morning, but by noon, when he was sweating through his undershirt despite the cold, his arms ached from the burden.

Leksi, along with all of his school friends, had eagerly anticipated enlistment. From the age of fourteen on, every girl in his class had been mad for the soldiers. Soldiers carried guns, wore uniforms, drove military vehicles. Their high black boots gleamed when they crossed their legs in the outdoor cafés. If you were eighteen and you weren't a soldier, you were a woman; if you were neither soldier nor woman, you were a cripple. Leksi had not been back to his hometown since enlisting. He wondered when he'd get to cross his legs at an outdoor café and raise his glass to the giggling girls.

Instead he had this: snow, snow, more snow, snow. It all looked the same to Leksi, and it was endless. He never paid attention to where they were going; he just followed the older soldiers. If he were ever to look up and find them gone, Leksi would be lost in the wilderness, without any hope of finding his way out. He could not understand why anyone would want to live here, let alone fight for the place.

He had first seen the Chechen highlands a month before, when the convoy carrying his infantry division across the central Caucasus stopped at the peak of the Daryal Pass so that the men could relieve themselves. The soldiers stood in a long line by the side of the road, jumping up and down like madmen, pissing into the wind, hollering threats and curses at their hidden enemies in the vast snowy distance.

He had been cold that afternoon, he had been cold every morning and night since then, he was cold now. He was so cold his teeth were cold. If he breathed through his mouth his throat hurt; if he breathed through his nose his head hurt. But he was the youngest, and he was a soldier, so he never complained.

Surkhov and Nikolai, on the other hand, never stopped complaining. They shouted to each other throughout the morning, back and forth. Leksi knew that armed guerrillas lurked in these hills; he heard they were paid a bounty for each enemy they brought to their chief, the *vor v zakone*, the "thief-in-power." The bodies of Russian soldiers were sometimes found crucified on telephone poles, their genitalia stuffed into their mouths. Their severed heads were left on the doorsteps of ethnic Russians in Grozny and Vladikavkaz. Leksi couldn't understand why Surkhov and Nikolai were so recklessly loud, but they had been soldiers for years. Both had seen extensive combat. Leksi didn't question them.

"Put Khlebnikov in charge," Surkhov was saying now, "and he'd clean this place up in two weeks. There's twelve pigfuckers here that tell all the other pigfuckers what to do. You put Khlebnikov in charge, he'd get the twelve, *ping ping ping.*" Surkhov made a gun with his thumb and forefinger and fired at the invisible twelve. He wasn't wearing gloves. Neither was Nikolai. Leksi got colder just looking at their bare red hands.

Surkhov was skinny but tireless. He could tramp through deep snow for hours without break, bitching and singing the whole way. His face seemed asymmetrical, one eye slightly higher than the other. It made him look perpetually skeptical. His shaggy brown hair spilled out from below his white watch cap. The caps were reversible—black on the inside for nighttime maneuvers. Leksi, whose head was still shaved to regulation specifications, felt vulnerable without his helmet, which he had left behind after Surkhov and Nikolai kept throwing pebbles at it. None of the older soldiers wore helmets. Helmets were considered unmanly, like seat belts, fit only for U.N. observers and French journalists.

Nikolai's hair was even longer than Surkhov's. Nikolai looked like an American movie star, strong-boned and blue-eyed, until he opened his mouth, which was jumbled with crooked teeth. If the teeth bothered him, it didn't show—he was constantly flashing his snaggletoothed smile, as if daring people to point out the gaps. Nobody ever did.

"They'll never bring Khlebnikov here," said Nikolai. "You're always talking Khlebnikov this, Khlebnikov that, so what? Never. Khlebnikov is a tank. They don't want tanks here. This"—and here Nikolai gestured at himself and Surkhov, their march, ignoring Leksi—"this is not *relevant*. This is a *game*. You want to know the truth? Moscow is happier if we die. If we die, all the newspapers rant about it, the politicians go on TV and rant about it, and then, maybe, they begin to fight for real."

Whenever Nikolai or Surkhov said the word *Moscow* it sounded profane. Actual curses rolled from their tongues, free and easy, but to *Moscow* they added the venom of a true malediction. Most of the older soldiers spoke the same way, and the intensity of their emotion surprised Leksi. Nikolai and Surkhov took almost nothing seriously. Surkhov would read aloud the letters he got from his girlfriend, affecting a high-pitched, quavering voice: "I long for you, darling, I wake in the morning and already long for you," and then he and Nikolai would burst into laughter. One night Nikolai described his father's long, excruciating death from bone cancer, and then shrugged, sipping from a mug of coffee spiked with vodka. "Well, he outlived his welcome."

A week ago they had been marching down an unpaved road. They walked in the tracks of an armored personnel carrier because the grooved and flattened snow gave better traction. They came across a skinny dead dog, and Surkhov dragged it by its front paws into the center of the road. Blackbirds had pecked out the eyes and testes. Surkhov, one hand on the back of its neck, lifted the dog's frozen corpse onto its hind legs and used it as a ventriloquist's dummy to sing, in falsetto, the old Zhana Matveyeva song.

"Why do you walk away, my darling, why do you walk away? I only have eyes for you, my darling, I only have eyes for you."

Nikolai had laughed, bent over at the waist, hands on his knees, laughing until the blackbirds circling overhead winged away. Leksi had smiled, because it would be rude not to smile, but he could not look away from the dog's eyeless face. Someone had shot it in the forehead; the bullet hole was round as a coin. One of the soldiers from the APC, taking target practice.

Leksi was deeply superstitious. His grandmother had taught him that the world was full of animals and that the animals all knew each other. There were secret conferences in the wild where the affairs of each beast were discussed and argued. A boy in his school had pegged a pigeon with a slingshot, killing it instantly. A year later the boy's older sister died in a car accident. Leksi did not believe it was an accident; he was sure the other birds had conspired and gained their revenge.

"Aleksandr!"

Leksi looked up from the snow and realized that he had fallen far behind Nikolai. He rushed forward, nearly tripping. Carrying the rifle disrupted his balance. When he was again ten meters behind the older soldier, he stopped and nodded, but Nikolai summoned him forward with curling fingers. Surkhov squatted down and observed them from his position, grinning.

"Who's watching my back?" asked Nikolai, when Leksi approached him.

"Me. I'm sorry."

"No, again, who's watching my back?"

"Me."

Nikolai shook his head and looked at Surkhov for a moment, who shrugged. "Nobody's watching my back," said

Nikolai. "You're watching the snow, you're watching the dogs, you're watching the sky. So, okay, you are an artist, I think. You are composing a painting, maybe, in your head. I appreciate this. But then tell me, if you are making this painting, who is watching my back?"

"Nobody."

"Ah. This is a problem. You see, I am watching Surkhov's back. Nobody can attack Surkhov from behind, because I would protect him. But who protects me? While you paint this masterpiece, who protects me?"

"Sorry."

"I will not die in this shit land, Aleksandr. You understand? I refuse to die here. You guard me, I guard Surkhov, we all live another day. You see?"

"Yes."

"Watch my back."

Only after they began marching again, after Surkhov and Nikolai began singing Beatles songs, replacing the original lyrics with obscene variations, did Leksi wonder who was watching *his* back.

· · ·

The three soldiers stopped less than a kilometer downhill of the mansion, at the edge of a dense copse of pines. A high wall of mortared stones surrounded the property; only the shingled roof and chimneys were visible from the soldiers' vantage point. A long field of snow lay between them and the house. The shadows of the tall trees stretched up the field in the last minutes of sunlight.

Surkhov took the binoculars back from Leksi and stared

through them. "They can watch the entire valley from there. No smoke from the chimneys. But they know we'd be looking for smoke."

Nikolai had pulled a plastic bag of tobacco and papers from Surkhov's pack; he leaned against a tree trunk now and rolled a cigarette. Leksi could roll a decent number if he were warm and indoors, sitting down, the paper flat on a tabletop. He was always amazed that Nikolai could roll them anywhere, in less than a minute, never dropping a flake of tobacco, no matter the wind or the darkness. Nikolai could roll a cigarette while driving a car over a dirt road and singing along with the radio.

He gripped the finished product between his lips while returning the plastic bag to Surkhov's pack. Leksi lit it for him and Nikolai inhaled hungrily, his stubbled cheeks caving in. He released the smoke and passed the cigarette to Leksi.

"Intelligence said no lights in the house the last three nights," said Nikolai.

Surkhov spat. "Intelligence couldn't find my cock if it was halfway up their ass. Fuck them and their patron saints. Aleshkovsky told me some of them flew a copter to Pitsunda last weekend, for the whores. We're down here freezing our balls off and they go whoring."

"So," said Nikolai, "they send three men. The way they see it, *A*, the place is empty, we take it, fine, we have a good observation post for the valley. *B*, half the terrorist army is in there, we're dead, fine. All at once, we are relevant. We are martyrs. The real fighting begins."

"I don't want to be relevant," said Leksi, handing the cigarette to Surkhov. The older soldiers looked at him quizzically for a moment and then laughed. It took Leksi a second to realize they were laughing with him, not at him.

"No," said Nikolai, clapping him on the back. "Neither do I."

After nightfall they unrolled their sleeping bags and slept in turns, one man always keeping watch. Leksi pulled the first shift but could not sleep after Nikolai relieved him. Every few minutes a dog would howl and then his brothers would answer, until the hills echoed with lonely dogs calling for each other. An owl screeched from a perch nearby. Leksi lay in his bag and stared up through the pine branches. A half-moon lit the sky and he watched the silhouetted clouds drift in and out of sight. He lay with his knees pressed against his chest for warmth and flinched every time the wind blew a stray pine needle against his cheek. He listened to Nikolai puffing on another hand-rolled cigarette and to Surkhov grinding his teeth in his sleep.

In a few hours he might be fighting for a house he had never seen before tonight, against men he had never met. He hadn't insulted anyone or fucked anyone's girlfriend, he hadn't stolen any money or crashed into anyone's car, and yet these men, if they were here, would try to kill him. It seemed very bizarre to Leksi. Strangers wanted to kill him. They didn't even know him, but they wanted to kill him. As if everything he had done was completely immaterial, everything he held in his mind: the girls he had kissed; the hunting trips with his father; the cow he had drawn for his mother when he was seven, still hanging in a frame on her bedroom wall; or the time he got caught sneaking glances over Katya Zubritskaya's shoulder during a geometry test, and old Lukonin had made him stand up right there and repeat, louder and louder while the students laughed and pounded their desks: *I am Aleksandr Strelchenko and I am a cheat, and not even a good cheat.* These memories were Aleksandr Strelchenko's, and so what? None of it mattered. None of it was real except here, now, the snow, the soldiers beside him, the house on the hilltop. Why did they need the house? To observe the valley. What was there to observe? Trees and snow and wild dogs, the Caucasus mountains looming in the distance. Leksi curled up inside his sleeping bag and pictured his severed head resting on a Grozny doorstep, his eyes the eyes of a dead fish on its bed of ice.

The midnight shift would have just started at the bottling plant back home where his older brother worked. If Leksi hadn't joined the army he would be there now, inside a warm building with dusty lead-glass windows, the overhead lights soft and yellow and steady. Maybe a conveyor belt had broken and Leksi was asked to fix it; he saw himself replacing a cracked roller and then regrooving the rubber belt. A radio played softly and Leksi chatted with the foreman about politics. Everyone knew everyone else; they had all grown up together. There were friends and there were enemies but everyone had their reasons. He would like Bobo, say, because Bobo was the goalie for their hockey club; he would hate Timur because Timur's wife was very beautiful and Timur wore tight Levi jeans that his brother sent him from America. That would be logical. That would be a life that made sense. And maybe at night he would dream of adventure, of sleeping in the snow with his rifle by his side, of storming hilltop houses and battling the Chechen terrorists, but it would just be a dream, and in the morning he would drink his coffee and read the newspaper and cluck sadly to learn that three more boys were killed in Chechnya.

. . .

At three A.M. they climbed the hill. They left their packs behind, wrapped tightly in waterproof tarps and buried below the snow, marked with broken twigs and pinecones. The moon was bright enough to make flashlights unnecessary. Surkhov and Nikolai seemed like different people now; since waking they had barely spoken. They had blackened each other's faces and then Leksi's, pocketed their watches, reversed their caps.

They reached the stone wall and circled around to the back gate. If there were any guard dogs, they would have already begun barking. That was a good sign. They found the back gate unlocked, swinging back and forth in the wind, creaking. That was another good sign. They crept onto the property. The grounds were sprawling and unkempt. A white gazebo stood by an old well; the gazebo's roof sagged from the weight of the snow.

The house's large windows were trimmed in copper. No lights were on. The soldiers took positions by hand signal: Surkhov approached the back door while Nikolai and Leksi lay on their stomachs and aimed their rifles past him. Surkhov looked at them for a moment, shrugged, and turned the knob. The door opened.

Nobody was home. They attached their flashlights to their rifle barrels and split up to check both floors and the cellar, slowly, slowly, looking for the silver gleam of a trip-wire, the matte gray of a pancake mine. They searched under the beds, in the closets, the shower stalls, the wine racks in the cellar, the modern toilet's water tank. When Leksi opened the refrigerator he gasped. The light came on.

"Electricity," he whispered. He couldn't believe it. He walked over to the light switch and flicked it up. The kitchen shined, the yellow-tiled floor, the wood counters, the big black stove. Surkhov hurried in, his boots thundering on the tiles. He turned off the light and slapped Leksi in the face.

"Idiot," he said.

• • •

When the search was completed, Nikolai radioed their base. He listened to instructions for a moment, nodded impatiently, signed off, and looked up at the other two, who were gathered around him in the library. "So now we sit here and wait."

The walls were bookshelves, crowded with more books than they were meant to hold, vertical stacks of books on top of horizontal rows of books. Books were piled in corners, books lay scattered on the leather sofa, books leaned precariously on the marble fireplace mantel.

Leksi's face was still flushed from embarrassment. He knew that he had deserved the slap, that he had acted stupidly, but he was furious anyway. He imagined that Surkhov slapped his girlfriends that way if he caught them stealing money, and it burned Leksi to be treated with such disrespect, as if he were unworthy of a punch.

Nikolai watched him. "Look," he said, "you understand why Surkhov was angry?"

"Yes."

"Did you check the refrigerator before you opened it?" asked Nikolai. "Did you check to see if it was wired? And then you turn on the lights! Now everyone in the valley knows we are here. You need to pay attention. You never pay attention and it's going to get you killed, which is fine, but it's going to get us killed also, which is not fine."

Surkhov smiled. "Tell me you're sorry, Leksi, and I'll apologize, too. Come on. Give me your hand."

Leksi was unable to hold grudges. He extended his hand and said, "I'm sorry."

"Fool," said Surkhov, ignoring Leksi's hand. He and Nikolai laughed and walked out of the library.

· · ·

They washed off the face paint in a blue-tiled bathroom, using soap shaped like seashells, drying themselves with green hand towels. Afterward they searched the rooms for loot. Leksi took the second floor, happy to be alone for a while, pointing his flashlight at everything that interested him. In one grand room, where he assumed the master of the house once slept, he stared in wonder at the bed. It was the biggest bed he had ever seen. He and his older brother had slept in a bed one third this size until his brother got married.

Blue porcelain lamps stood on the night tables. A teacup sat on a saucer beneath one of these lamps. The cup's rim was smudged with red lipstick, and some tea had spilled into the saucer.

A heavy black dresser with brass handles stood against one wall. On top of the dresser were pill bottles, a brush tangled with long gray hairs, a china bowl filled with coins, a cut-glass vial of perfume, a jar of pungent face cream, and several silver-framed photographs. One of the photographs caught Leksi's eye, an old black-and-white, and he picked it up. A raven-haired woman stared at the camera. She looked faintly bored yet willing to play along, the same expression Leksi saw on all the beautiful young wives in his hometown. Her dark eyebrows plunged toward each other but didn't meet.

Leksi had the eerie sense, examining the photograph, that the woman knew she would be seen this way. As if she expected that a day would come, years and years after the shutter clicked, when a stranger with a rifle strapped to his shoulder would point his flashlight at her face and wonder what her name was.

He checked the other rooms on the floor and then went downstairs, not realizing that he was still holding the framed photograph until he entered the dark library. He saw a match flare and he pointed his flashlight in that direction. Surkhov and Nikolai were sprawled on the leather sofa, their boots and socks kicked off, their stinking bare feet on the glass-topped coffee table. They had removed their parkas and sweaters; their undershirts were mottled with sweat stains. They were smoking cigars. On the floor beside them was a heap of silver that glowed cool and lunar when Leksi aimed his flashlight at it: serving trays and candlesticks,

tureens and ladles, napkin rings and decanters. Leksi wondered how they expected to carry all that loot home with
them. Maybe they didn't, maybe they just liked the sight of
it, the piled treasure. A two-foot-tall blond china doll wearing a white nightdress sat on Nikolai's lap. His hand was
massaging the doll's thighs. He winked at Leksi.

"Aren't you hot?"

It was true; Leksi was hot. He had been cold for so long
that the heat had been welcome, but now he leaned his rifle
against a bookcase, carefully set the photograph on the mantel, and shrugged out of his parka.

"They must have run off in a hurry," said Surkhov. "Left
the electricity on, left the heat on." He inspected the glowing
ash on the tip of his cigar. "Left the cigars."

Nikolai leaned forward and lifted a wood cigar box off the
coffee table. "Here," he said to Leksi. "Take your pick."

Leksi selected a cigar, bit off the end, lit it, and lay down
on the rug in front of the dead fireplace. He turned off his
flashlight. They puffed away in the darkness and did not
speak for a time. It was very good to lie there, in the warm
house, smoking a good cigar. They listened to the wind gust-
ing outside. Leksi felt safer than he had in weeks. The other
two were tough on him, it was true, but they knew what
they were doing. They were making him a better soldier.

"Leksi," said Surkhov, sleepily. "Leksi."

"Yes?"

"When you opened the refrigerator, what did you see?"

Leksi thought this was probably another trick. "Look," he
said, "I'm sorry about the—"

"No, what was inside the refrigerator? Did you get a look?"

"Lots of stuff. A chicken."

"A chicken," said Surkhov. "Cooked or uncooked?"

"Cooked."

"Did it look good?"

For some reason Leksi thought this was a very funny question and he began to laugh. Nikolai laughed, too, and soon all three of them were shaking with laughter.

"Ay me," said Nikolai, sucking his cigar back to life.

"No really," said Surkhov. "Did it look like it'd been sitting there for months?"

"No. It looked very good, actually."

Leksi lay on his back with his hands behind his head and thought about the chicken. Then he thought about his feet. He unlaced his boots and pulled them off, and the wet socks as well. He shone his flashlight on his toes and wiggled them. They were all there. He hadn't seen them in a long time.

"Well," said Surkhov, sitting up. "Let's get that chicken."

. . .

They ate off bone-china plates, with silver forks and wood-handled knives, at the long dining room table. The sun was beginning to rise. The crystal chandelier above the table refracted the light and created multicolored patterns on the pale blue wallpaper. Nikolai's blond doll sat in the seat next to him.

The roasted chicken was dry from sitting in the refrigerator, but not spoiled. They chewed the bones, sucking out the marrow. The soldiers had found a nearly full bottle of vodka in the freezer and they drank from heavy tumblers, staring out the windows at the valley that opened before them.

The snow and trees, the frozen lake in the distance, everything looked beautiful, harmonious and pure. Nikolai spotted an eagle and pointed it out; they all watched the bird soar high above the valley floor. When they were finished eating they pushed the plates to the center of the table and leaned back in their chairs, rubbing their bellies. They exchanged a volley of burps and grinned at one another.

"So Aleksandr," said Nikolai, picking at his teeth with his thumbnail. "You have a girlfriend?"

Leksi took another drink and let the alcohol burn in his mouth for a moment before answering. "Not really."

"What does this mean, 'not really'?"

"It means no."

"But you've been with women?"

Leksi burped and nodded. "Here and there."

"Virgin," said Surkhov, carving his name into the mahogany tabletop with his knife.

"No," said Leksi, undefiantly. He was not a liar and people eventually figured this out. Right now he was too warm and well-fed to be goaded into irritation. "I've been with three girls."

Nikolai raised his eyebrows as if the number impressed him. "You must be a legend in your hometown."

"And I've kissed eleven."

Surkhov plunged his knife into the table and shouted, "That's a lie!" Then he giggled and drank more vodka.

"Eleven," repeated Leksi.

"Are you counting your mother?" Surkhov asked.

"I'm a very good kisser," said Leksi. "They all said so."

Nikolai and Surkhov looked at each other and laughed. "Excellent," said Nikolai. "We're lucky to have such an expert with us. Could you demonstrate?" He reached over and grabbed the doll by its hair and tossed it to Leksi, who caught it and looked into its blue-glass eyes.

"I don't like blondes," said Leksi. The other men laughed and Leksi was very pleased with the joke. He laughed himself and took another drink.

"Please," said Nikolai. "Teach us."

Leksi supported the doll by the back of its head and leaned forward to kiss its painted porcelain lips. He kept his eyes closed. He thought about the last real girl he had kissed, the eleventh, the night before entering the army.

When Leksi opened his eyes Nikolai was standing, hands on his hips, frowning. "No," he said. "Where is the passion?" He grabbed the doll by the shoulders and pulled it from Leksi's hands. He stared angrily at the doll's face. "Who do you love, doll? Is it Aleksandr? No? Is it me? I don't believe you. How can I trust you?" He cupped the doll's face in his palms and kissed it mightily.

Leksi was impressed. It was a much better kiss, there was no question. He wanted another chance but Nikolai tossed the doll aside. It landed on its back on the oaken sideboard. Surkhov clapped and whistled, as if Nikolai had just scored the winning goal for their club team.

"That is a kiss," said Nikolai, wiping his lips with the back of his hand. "You must always kiss as if kissing will be outlawed at dawn." He seized the vodka bottle from the table and saw that it was empty. "Surkhov! You drunk bastard, you finished it!"

Surkhov nodded. "Good vodka."

Nikolai stared sadly through the bottle. "There was more in the freezer?"

"No."

"There's all that wine in the cellar," said Leksi, looking at the doll's little black shoes dangling over the sideboard's edge.

"Yes!" said Nikolai. "The cellar."

Leksi followed Nikolai down the narrow staircase, both of them still barefoot. The cellar was windowless so Nikolai turned on the lights. The corners of the room were cob-webbed. A billiards table covered with a plastic sheet stood against one wall. A chalkboard above it still tallied the score from an old game. In the middle of the floor a yellow toy dump truck sat on its side. Leksi picked it up and rolled its wheels; it would make a good gift for his little nephew.

One entire wall was a wine rack, a giant honeycomb of clay-colored octagonal cubbies. Foil-wrapped bottle tops peeked out of each. Nikolai pulled one bottle out and inspected the label.

"French." He handed it to Leksi. "The French are the whores of Europe, but they make nice wine." He pulled out two more bottles and they turned to go. They were halfway up the stairs when Nikolai placed his two wine bottles on the step above him, drew his pistol from his waist holster, and chambered a bullet. Leksi did not have a pistol. His rifle was still in the library. He held a bottle in one hand and the toy truck in the other. He looked at Nikolai, not sure what was happening.

"Leksi," whispered Nikolai. "How do they play pool with the table jammed against the wall?"

Leksi shook his head. He had no idea what the older man was talking about.

"Get Surkhov. Get your rifles and come down here."

By the time Leksi had retrieved Surkhov from the dining room, their rifles from the library, and returned to the cellar staircase, Nikolai was gone. Then they heard him calling for them. "Come on, come on, it's over."

They found him standing above an opened trapdoor, his pistol reholstered. He had shoved the billiards table aside to get to the trapdoor, a feat of strength that Leksi did not even register until a few minutes later. The three soldiers stared down into the tiny subcellar. An old woman sat on a bare mattress. She did not look up at them. Her thinning gray hair was tied back in a bun and her spotted hands trembled on her knees. She wore a long black dress. A black cameo on a slender silver chain hung from her neck. Aside from the mattress, a small table holding a hot plate was the only furniture. A pyramid of canned food sat against one wall, next to several plastic jugs of water. A short aluminum stepladder leaned against another wall.

"Is this your house, Grandmother?" asked Surkhov. The woman did not respond.

"She's not talking," said Nikolai. He crouched down, grabbed the edge of the door frame, and lowered himself into the bunker. The woman did not look at him. Nikolai patted her for weapons, gently but thoroughly. He kicked over the pyramid of cans, checked under the hot plate, knocked on the walls to make sure they were not hollow.

"All right," he said. "Let's get her out of here. Come on, Grandmother, up." The woman did not move. He grabbed her by the elbows and hoisted her into the air. Surkhov and Leksi reached down; each grabbed an arm and pulled her up. Nikolai climbed out of the bunker; all three men stood around the old woman and stared at her.

She looked back at them now, her amber eyes wide and furious. Leksi recognized her. She had been the young woman in the photograph.

"This is *my* house," she said in Russian, looking at each man in turn. She had a thick Chechen accent but she articulated each word clearly. "*My* house," she repeated.

"Yes, Grandmother," said Nikolai. "We are your guests. Please, come upstairs with us."

She seemed bewildered by his polite tone, and let them lead her to the staircase. When Nikolai retrieved his wine bottles she pointed at them. "That is not your wine," she said. "Put it back."

He nodded and handed the bottles to Leksi. "Put them back where we got them."

When Leksi came upstairs he heard them talking in the library. He went there and found the old woman sitting on the sofa, rubbing her black cameo between her fingers. It was hard to believe that she had once been beautiful. The loose skin of her face and throat was furrowed and mottled. At her feet was the piled silver, glittering in the sunlight that poured through the windows.

Surkhov had pulled a leather-bound book from a shelf

and was skimming through it, licking his fingertips each time he turned a page. Nikolai sat on the floor across from the woman, his back against the marble side of the fireplace. He held an iron poker in his hands. The silver-framed photograph still rested on the mantel. Leksi waited in the doorway, wondering if the old woman saw her picture. He wished he had never moved it. There was something terribly shameful about forcing the beautiful young woman to witness her future. The vodka, which Leksi had drunk with such pleasure a few minutes ago, now burned in his stomach.

"Don't do that," said the old woman. The soldiers looked at her. "This," she said angrily, licking her fingertips in imitation of Surkhov. "You will ruin the paper."

Surkhov nodded, smiled at her, and returned the book to its shelf. Nikolai stood, still holding the poker, and gestured to Leksi. He ushered him out to the hallway and closed the library doors behind them. They went into the dining room. The dirty plates, littered with broken chicken bones, still sat in the middle of the table. Nikolai and Leksi looked out the high window at the snow-covered valley.

Nikolai sighed. "It is not a pleasant thing, but she is old. Her life from now on would be very bad. Give her back to her Allah."

Leksi turned and stared at the older soldier. "Me?"

"Yes," said Nikolai, spinning the poker in his hands. "It is very important that you do it. Have you shot anyone before?"

"No."

"Good. She will be the first. I know, Aleksandr, you don't want to kill an old woman. None of us do. But think. Being a soldier is not about killing the people you want to kill. It would be nice, wouldn't it? If we only shot the people we hated. This woman, she is the enemy. She has bred enemies, and they will breed more. She buys them guns and food, and they slaughter our men. These people," he said, pointing at the ceiling above them, "they are the richest people in the region. They have funded the terrorists for years. They sleep in their silk sheets while the mines they paid for blow our friends' legs off. They drink their French wine while their bombs explode in our taverns, our restaurants. She is not innocent."

Leksi started to say something but Nikolai shook his head and lightly tapped Leksi's arm with the poker. "No, this is not something to discuss. This is not a conversation we are having. Take her outside and shoot her. Not on the property, I don't want the blackbirds coming here. Bad luck. Take her into the woods and shoot her and bury her."

They were quiet for a minute, watching the distant lake, watching the wind-blown snow swirl above the pine trees. Finally Leksi asked, "How old were you? The first time?"

"The first time I shot someone? Nineteen."

Leksi nodded and opened his mouth, but forgot what he had meant to say. Finally he asked, "Who were we fighting back then?"

Nikolai laughed. "How old do you think I am, Aleksandr?"

"Thirty-five?"

Nikolai smiled broadly, flashing his crooked teeth. "Twenty-four." He pressed the poker's tip against the base of Leksi's skull. "Here's where the bullet goes."

. . .

When they brought her into the house's mudroom and told her to put on her boots, she stared up at the soldiers, her hands trembling by her side. For a long while she stared at them, and Leksi wondered what they would have done to her if she had still been young and beautiful. And then he wondered what they would do if she simply refused to put her boots on. How could they threaten her? Would they shoot her there and carry her into the woods? He hoped that would happen, that she would fall down on the floor and refuse to rise, and Nikolai or Surkhov would be forced to shoot her. But she didn't, she simply stared at them and finally nodded, as though she were agreeing with something. She sat on the bench by the door and pulled on a pair of fur-lined boots. They seemed too big for her, as if she were a child trying on her mother's boots. She tucked the black cameo on its silver chain inside her dress and pulled on a fur coat made from the dark pelts of some animal Leksi could not name.

A heavy snow shovel hung on the wall, blade up, between two pegs. Surkhov took it down and handed it to the old woman. She grabbed it from him and headed out the door without a word. Leksi looked at his two comrades, hoping they would tell him it was all a prank, that nobody would be killed today. Nikolai would punch him on the arm and tell him he was a fool, and everyone would laugh; the old woman would pop back into the mudroom, laughing—she was in on it, it was a great practical joke. But Surkhov and Nikolai stood there, still barefoot, their faces expressionless, waiting for him to leave. Leksi walked out the door and closed it behind him.

The old woman dragged the shovel behind her as if it were a sled. The snow came up to her knees; she had to stop every minute for a rest. She would take several deep breaths and then continue walking, the shovel's blade bouncing over her footprints. She never looked back. Leksi followed three paces behind, rifle in hand. He followed her out the back gate and told her to turn right, and she did, and they circled to the front of the property and then down the hill.

Every time she stopped, Leksi would stare at the back of her head, at the gray bun held in place with hairpins, with growing fury. Why had she stayed behind in the house when everyone else had left? She hadn't been abandoned. Somebody had helped her down into the subcellar; somebody had dragged the billiards table over the trapdoor. It must have been pure greed, a refusal to give up the trinkets she had accumulated over the years, her crystal and her silver and her French wine and the rest. The others must have urged her to come with them. She was stubborn; she would not listen to reason; she was a fanatic.

"Why did you stay here?" he finally asked. He had not meant to speak with her; the question came out unbidden.

She turned slowly and stared up at him. "It is *my* house," she said. "Why did *you* come?"

"All right," he said, pointing the rifle at her. "Keep moving." He did not expect her to obey him, but she did. They were walking down to where the three soldiers had hidden their packs, about a kilometer away; Leksi would carry them back up and save Surkhov and Nikolai a trip. It would be hard going, carrying three packs uphill, but he thought it would be much better than this walk downhill. Because Leksi did not doubt for a second that what he was doing now was a sin. This was evil. He was going to shoot an old woman in the back of the head, watch her pitch forward into the snow, and then bury her. There was nothing to call it but evil.

He had long suspected that he was a coward. His older brother would tell him ghost stories in the night and Leksi would lie awake for hours after. Sometimes he would shake his brother awake and make him promise that the stories were lies. And his brother would say, "Of course, Leksi, of course, just stories," and hold his hand until he fell asleep.

"They chose you because you are the baby," said the old woman, and Leksi squinted to look at her through the glare of sunlight reflecting off the snow.

"Just walk."

She hadn't stopped walking, though, and she continued talking. "It's a test for you. They want to see how strong you are."

Leksi said nothing, just watched the shovel skip down the slope.

"They don't care if I live or die, you must know this. Why should they? Look at me, what can I do? They are testing you. Can't you see this? You are smart, you must see."

"No," said Leksi. "I'm not smart."

"Neither am I. But I've lived with men for seventy years. I understand men. Right now, they are watching us."

Leksi looked up the hill, to the mansion at its crown. He

suspected she was right, that Nikolai was watching them through his binoculars. When he turned back the old woman was still trudging forward, her breath rising in vapors above her head. She seemed to be moving more easily now, and Leksi decided that she was in better shape than she had pretended, that her constant pauses were not caused by exhaustion but rather by an attempt to delay what was going to happen. He understood that. He, too, dreaded the ending.

"But at the bottom of the hill," the old woman said, "they won't be able to see us. That is where you can let me go. They expect you to. If they wanted you to kill me, would they have let you go by yourself? Why would they want you to take me so far away, out of sight?"

"They don't want the blackbirds to come near the house," said Leksi, and when he said it he realized it made no sense. He was going to bury her. Why would the blackbirds come? Besides, Nikolai was not a superstitious man.

The old woman laughed, the gray bun at the back of her head bobbing up and down. "The blackbirds? That is what they said, the blackbirds? This is only a joke, boy. Wake up! They are playing with you."

"Grandmother," said Leksi, but he couldn't think of anything else to say. She stopped and turned again to stare at him, smiling. She still had all her teeth but they were yellowed and long. The sight of the teeth infuriated Leksi; he rushed down the hill and jabbed the muzzle of his rifle into her stomach.

"Keep walking!" he yelled at her.

When they were halfway from the bottom she asked, "How will my grandchildren know where to come?"

"What?"

"When they come to visit my grave, how will they know where it is?"

"I'll put a marker up," said Leksi. He had no intention of putting a marker up, but how else could he answer such a question? His fury had already disappeared and he was disgusted with himself for letting it go so quickly.

"Now?" she asked. "What's the good of that? When the snow melts the marker will fall."

"I'll put one up in the spring." He knew this must sound as ridiculous to the woman as it did to him, but if she thought his assurance was preposterous she gave no sign.

"With my name on it," said the old woman. "Tamara Shashani." She spelled both names and then made Leksi repeat it.

Leksi had known a girl named Tamara in school. She was fat and freckled and laughed like a braying donkey. It seemed impossible that this woman and that girl could share a name.

"And my hometown," added the old woman. "Put that on the marker, too. Djovkhar Ghaala."

"You mean Grozny."

"No, I mean Djovkhar Ghaala. I was born there, I know the name."

Leksi shrugged. He had been in the city four days ago. The Chechens called it Djovkhar Ghaala; the Russians called it Grozny; the Chechens had been driven out; the city was Grozny.

"Tell me," said the old woman. "Do you remember everything?"

"Tamara Shashani. From Djovkhar Ghaala."

Leksi followed behind her, eyes half closed. The sunlight's glare was making his head hurt. The shovel's blade carved a little trail in the snow and he tried to step only in that trail, not sure why it mattered but anxious not to stray outside the parallel lines.

"Do you know the story of when the Devil came to Orekhovo?"

"No," said Leksi.

"It's an old story. My grandfather told me when I was a girl. The Devil was lonely. He wanted a bride. He wanted company for his palace in Hell."

From the manner in which the old woman spoke, Leksi knew that she had told the tale many times before. She never paused for thought; she never needed to search for the right phrase. He pictured her sitting on the edge of her children's beds, and then her grandchildren, reciting their favorite adventure, the story of when the Devil came to Orekhovo.

"So he gathered his minions, all the demons that wandered through the world spreading discord. He brought them into the meeting hall and asked them to name the most beautiful woman alive. Naturally, the demons argued for hours. They never agreed on anything. Brawls broke out as each championed his favorite. The Devil watched, bored, tapping his long nails on the armrest of his throne. But finally, after tails had been chopped off and horns broken, one of the senior demons stepped forward and announced that they had chosen. Her name was Aminah, and she lived in the town of Orekhovo."

Leksi smiled. He had heard this story before, except that in the version he knew the beautiful woman lived in Petrikov and was called Tatyana. He tried to remember who had told him the story.

"So the Devil mounted his great black horse and rode to Orekhovo. It was a winter's day. When he got there he asked a child he met on the road where the beautiful Aminah lived. After the boy gave directions the Devil grabbed him by the collar, slashed his throat, plucked out his blue eyes, and pocketed them. He threw the boy's body into a ditch and continued on his way."

Leksi remembered that part. Don't talk to strangers, that was the lesson. He looked uphill and saw that the mansion was no longer in view. If he did let the woman go, who would know? But she would seek out her people and tell them that three Russians had occupied her house. Perhaps there would be a counterattack, and Leksi would die knowing that he had orchestrated his own doom.

"When the Devil found Aminah's house, he hitched his horse to a post and knocked on the door. A fat woman opened it and invited him inside, for the Devil was dressed like a gentleman. She stirred a pot of stew that bubbled above the fire. 'What are you seeking, traveler?' she asked. 'I seek Aminah,' said the Devil. 'I have heard of her great beauty.'

" 'She is my daughter,' said the fat woman. 'Have you come to ask for her hand? Many suitors wait upon her, yet she has refused all. What do you have to offer?' The Devil pulled out a purse and undid the strings. He dumped a pile of gold coins onto the floor. 'Ay,' said Aminah's mother, 'At last

I am wealthy! Go to her, she is at the lake. Tell her I approve of your suit.' When the woman sat on the floor and began counting her gold, the Devil crept up behind her and slashed her throat. He plucked out her blue eyes and pocketed them. He ladled himself a bowl of stew and ate until he was full, and then he left the house and mounted his black horse."

Never invite a stranger into the house, thought Leksi. And never count your gold while someone stands behind you. The more he considered it, the more he doubted that the Chechens would attack the house. Why should they? Any direct assault would result in a quick reprisal, so they couldn't keep the house if they did take it. There was too much risk involved for such a cheap reward: three Russian soldiers without vehicles or artillery.

"The Devil came to the lake and saw his prize. His demons had done well: Aminah was more beautiful than all the angels the Devil had once consorted with. The lake was frozen over and Aminah sat on the ice pulling on her skates. 'Good afternoon,' said the Devil. 'May I join you?' Aminah nodded, for the Devil was handsome and dressed like a gentleman. He walked back to his horse, opened his saddlebag, and pulled out a pair of skates, shined black leather, the blades gleaming and sharp."

When Leksi listened to the story as a child he asked how the Devil had known to bring his skates. Whom had he asked? His mother! He could picture it now; she was sitting at the edge of the bed while Leksi and his brother fought for the blanket. He asked how the Devil knew to bring the skates and his brother groaned and called him an idiot. But his mother nodded as if it were a very wise question. He could have pulled anything from that saddlebag, she told Leksi. It was the Devil's saddlebag. If he had needed a trombone he would have found it there.

"Aminah watched the Devil carefully," continued the old woman. "She watched him sit down on the ice and pull off his boots, and she saw his cloven hooves. She looked away quickly, so he would not catch her spying. They skated out to the center of the lake. The Devil was fantastic. He carved perfect figure eights, he pirouetted gracefully, he sped across the ice and jumped and spun through the air. When he returned to Aminah's side he pulled a necklace of great blue diamonds from his pocket. 'This is yours,' he told her, placing it around her neck and fastening the clasp. 'Now come with me to my country, where I am king. I will make you my queen, and you will never work again. All of my people will bow before you, they will scatter rose petals before your feet wherever you walk. Anything that you desire will be yours, except this: When you take my hand and come to my land, you can never go home.'"

Leksi and the old woman were walking in a narrow gully now, over slippery stones. Snow melted in the sun and streamed weakly over the rocks. It was treacherous footing but the old woman seemed to handle it with ease; she was agile as a goat.

"Aminah smiled and nodded and pretended that she was thinking about it. She skated away at a leisurely pace, and the Devil followed behind her. She skated and skated and the Devil pursued her, licking his sharp teeth with his forked tongue. But he did not know this lake, and Aminah did. She knew it in summer, when the fish leapt up to catch flies and moths, and she knew it in winter, when the ice was thick in some places and thin in others. She was a slender girl and the Devil was a big man; she hoped he was as heavy as he looked."

Listening to the story now and remembering how it ended, Leksi felt sorry for the Devil. Was the Devil really so terrible? True, he had murdered the innocent boy on the road. But Aminah's mother had deserved it for selling her daughter so cheaply. And what the Devil desired—who could blame him? He wanted to marry the world's most beautiful woman. What was wrong with that?

Just let the old woman go, thought Leksi. Just let her walk away. The odds are good she'll never make it to shelter before nightfall. I'd be giving her a chance, though, and what more could she ask of me? That would be mercy, to let her walk. But then Leksi thought of Nikolai. Nikolai would ask how it had gone and Leksi would be forced to lie. Except he could not imagine lying to Nikolai. Leksi never lied; he wasn't good at it. He pictured Nikolai's face and Leksi knew he could never trick the older soldier. And he could not go back to the mansion and admit that he had disobeyed a direct order.

"Finally Aminah could hear the ice beginning to crack beneath her skates. The Devil was right behind her, reaching out for her, his fingernails inches from her hair. Just as he was about to grab her the ice beneath him gave way and he fell with a cry into the freezing water. 'Aminah!' he yelled. 'Help me!' But Aminah skated away as fast as she could. She reached the edge of the lake, took off her skates, put her boots on, and left the town, never to return."

She kept the diamonds, thought Leksi. Maybe they turned back into eyeballs. He remembered being disappointed, as a child, that the Devil could be so easily trapped. Why couldn't he just breathe fire and melt all the ice?

The runoff from the melting snow had created a shallow stream in the gully that rose halfway up Leksi's boots. He worried about falling and twisting an ankle—how could he climb back uphill with a sprained ankle? Still, it was less exhausting than trudging through the wet snow. He remembered waking early on summer mornings with his brother, searching under rocks in the woods for slugs and beetles, pinning them on fishhooks, wading into the polluted river and casting their lines. They never caught anything, the waste from the nearby paper plant had poisoned the fish, but Leksi's brother would tell jokes all morning and then they would lie on the riverbank and talk about hockey stars who played in America and actresses on television.

"What happened next?" Leksi asked the old woman. He couldn't remember if there had been an epilogue.

The old woman stopped walking and looked skyward. A blackbird squawked on a pine branch above them. "Nobody knows. Some say the Devil swam under the ice and back to Hell. They say that every winter he returns, looking for Aminah, calling out her name."

The Devil really loved her, decided Leksi. He always rooted for the bad men in fairy tales and movies, not because he admired them but because they had no chance. The bad men were the true underdogs. They never won.

Leksi and the old woman stood motionless, their breath curling about their heads like genies. Leksi heard growls and turned to see where they came from. In the shadow of a great boulder twenty meters away three dogs feasted on a deer's still-steaming intestines. Each dog seemed to sense Leksi's gaze at the same time; they lifted their heads and stared at him until he averted his eyes.

Leksi looked uphill and realized they were no longer standing on a hill. Panicked, he searched for footprints, but there were none on the gully's wet stones. How long had they walked in the stream? Where had they entered it? All the tall pine trees looked identical to him; they stretched on for as far as the eye could see. Nothing but trees and melting snow littered with broken twigs and pinecones. The dogs watched him and the blackbird squawked and Leksi knew he was lost. He strapped the rifle over his shoulder, pulled off a glove, and began fumbling in his parka's pockets for his compass. The old woman turned to look at him and Leksi tried to remain as calm as possible. He pulled out the compass and peered at it. He determined true north and then closed his eyes. It didn't matter. He had no idea in which direction the house lay. Knowing true north meant nothing.

The old woman smiled at him when he opened his eyes. "It's an old story. Of course," she said, letting the shovel's long handle fall onto the wet rocks, "some people say there is no Devil."

Leksi sat on the bank of the now bustling stream. If he could organize his thoughts, he believed, everything would be all right. Unless he organized his thoughts he would die here in the nighttime, the snow would drift over his body and only the dogs would know where to find him. He stared at his lap to rest his eyes from the glare. Feeling hot, he laid his rifle on the ground and shrugged out of his parka. The sun was heavy on his face and he could feel his pale cheeks beginning to burn. He listened to the countryside around him: the dogs snarling at the blackbirds; the blackbirds flapping their wings; the running water; the pine branches creaking. He sat in the snow and listened to the countryside around him.

When he finally raised his head the old woman was gone, as he knew she would be. Her shovel was half-submerged in the stream, its handle wedged between two rocks, its metal blade glinting below water like the scale of a giant fish. The sun rose higher in the sky and the snow began to fall from the trees. Leksi stood, pulled on his parka, picked up his rifle, and started wading upstream, searching for the spot where his footprints ended.

He hadn't gone far when he heard a whistle. He crouched down, fumbling with the rifle, trying to get his gloved finger inside the trigger guard.

"Relax, Leksi." It was Nikolai, squatting by the trunk of a dead pine. The tree's bare branches reached out for the blue sky. Nikolai tapped off the ash of the cigar he was smoking. He was in shirtsleeves, his rifle strapped over one shoulder.

"You followed me," said Leksi.

The older soldier did not reply. He squinted into the distance beyond Leksi and Leksi followed his gaze, but there was nothing to be seen. A moment later a single gunshot echoed across the valley floor. Nikolai nodded, stood up, and stretched his arms above his head. He picked a bit of loose tobacco off his tongue and then tramped through the snow to the stream. Leksi, still in his crouch, watched him come closer.

Nikolai pulled the shovel out of the water and held it up. "Come over here, my friend."

Leksi heard singing behind him. He turned to find Surkhov marching toward them, singing "Here Comes the Sun," twirling a silver chain with a black cameo on its end.

Nikolai smiled and held out the shovel. "Come here, Aleksandr. You have work to do."

ZOANTHROPY

Whenever a lion was spotted prowling the avenues, the authorities contacted my father. He had a strange genius for tracking predators; he made a lifelong study of their habits; he never missed an open shot.

There is a statue of him in Carl Schurz Park, a hulking bronze. He stands, rifle slung casually over his shoulder, one booted foot atop a dead lion's haunches. A simple inscription is carved on the marble pedestal: *MacGregor Bonner / Defender of the City*. The statue's proportions are too heroic—no Bonner ever had forearms like that—but the sculptor caught the precise angle of my father's jawline, the flat bridge of his nose, the peacemaking eyes of a man who never missed an open shot.

In the old days, the media cooperated with the authorities—nobody wanted to spark a panic by publishing news of big cats in the streets. That attitude is long gone, of course. Every photographer in the country remembers the *New York Post*'s famous shot of the dead lion sprawled across the double yellow lines on Twenty-third Street, eyes rolled white, blood leaking from his open jaws, surrounded by grinning policemen, below the banner headline: "Bagged!" My father was the triggerman; the grinning policemen were there to keep the crowds away.

So it's sacrilege to admit, but I always rooted for the cats' escape. A treasonous confession, like a matador's son pulling for the bull, and I don't know what soured me on my father's business. A reverence for exiled kings, I suppose, for the fallen mighty. I wanted the lions to have a chance. I wanted them to live.

All good stories start on Monday, my father liked to say, a line he inherited from *his* father, a Glasgow-born minister who served as a chaplain for the British troops in North Africa and later moved to Rhodesia, where my father was born. For my grandfather, the only story worth reading was the holy one, King James Version. My father rejected the God of the book in favor of empirical truth. He never understood my obsession with fictions, the barbarians, starships, detectives, and cowboys that filled the shelves of my childhood room. He purged his mind of fantasy only to watch his lone child slip back into the muck.

This story starts on Tuesday. I was twenty years old. On bad afternoons I sometimes found myself where I had not meant to go: lying on the dead grass in Bryant Park with a bottle of celery soda balanced on my chest; inside a Chinese herb store breathing exotic dust; riding the subway to the end of the line, Far Rockaway, and back. The bad days came like Churchill's black dogs; they paced the corridor outside my bedroom, raking the carpet with their claws. The bad days chewed the corners. When my corners got too chewed for walking, I took a taxi to the Frick Museum, stood in front of Bellini's Saint Francis, and waited for the right angles to return.

On this bad Tuesday I stared at Saint Francis and Saint Francis stared into the sky, hands open by his side, head tilted back, lips parted, receiving the full favor of the Lord. Bellini shows the man at the moment of his stigmatization, the spots of blood sprouting from his palms. I don't think I'm being vulgar or inaccurate when I say that the saint's expression is orgasmic—the Rapture of divine penetration. The animals are waiting for him, the wild ass, the rabbit, the skinny-legged heron—they want to have a word with him, they see that Francis is in ecstasy and they're concerned. From the animal perspective, I think, nothing that makes you bleed is a good thing. The rabbit, especially, watches the proceedings with extreme skepticism.

After an hour things inside my brain sorted themselves out, the thoughts began to flow with relative order, my bladder swelled painfully. In the restroom, I locked myself in the toilet stall, did my business, closed the seat, and sat down for a smoke.

The stall walls were covered with names and dates, a worldly graffiti: Rajiv from London, Thiago from São Paulo, Sikorsky from Brooklyn.

Someone rapped on the door. "Occupied," I said.

"You'll have to put out the cigarette, sir. No smoking in the museum."

I took a final long drag, stood, lifted the toilet seat, and flushed the butt. When I opened the stall door the guard was still standing there, a tired-looking kid about my age, batwing-eared, narrow-shouldered, his maroon blazer two sizes too large. He stared at me sadly, hands in his pockets.

"You smoke Lucky Strikes," he said. "I could smell them from the hallway. They used to be my brand." He spoke with a forlorn air, as if the real meaning of his words were, *You slept with Cindy. She used to be my girlfriend.* "Hey," he added, smiling, "the Saint Francis man."

I squinted at him and he nodded happily.

"You're the guy who always comes and stands by that Saint Francis painting. What's the matter, you don't like the other stuff?"

"I like *The Polish Rider.*"

I was spending too much time in this place. The Frick made for a cheap afternoon with my student discount—I had dropped out of NYU after a term but kept my ID. I hated the idea that people were watching me. Perhaps I had grown too dependent on Saint Francis. I walked over to the sink to wash my hands.

"Me too, I like that one. Well, listen, sorry about busting you. It's pretty high school. Detention! But I've only been working here a couple weeks and, you know."

He held the door open for me and I thanked him, exited the bathroom, drying my hands on the seat of my corduroys. The guard followed me, walking with a bowlegged strut as though he had six-guns strapped to his waist. "The thing about Lucky Strikes, they have this sweetness, this . . . I don't know how to describe it."

"You're not from New York, are you?"

"Huh?"

"Where are you from?"

He grinned, jangling the heavy key ring dangling from his belt. "Bethlehem, Pennsylvania. What, I have hay in my hair?" His Bethlehem had two syllables: *beth-lem.*

We were in the garden courtyard now, a beautiful pillared room with an iron trelliswork skylight and a fountain in the center where stone frogs spitting water flanked a giant marble lily pad. I sat down on a bench and watched the frogs. The guard stood behind me, fiddling with his black tie. He seemed lonely. Or gay. Or both.

"So you're an artist?" I asked him. "You're in school here?"

"Nah. I don't think I could look at paint after being in this place all day. Nope, not for me."

"Actor?"

"Nope, nothing like that. It's—"

We both saw the lion at the same time, padding below the colonnade on the far side of the courtyard, yellow eyes glimmering in the shadows, claws click-clacking on the floor. He rubbed his side back and forth against a pillar before limping to the fountain. The lion looked unwell. His mane was tangled and matted down; an open red sore marred one shoulder; his ribs seemed ready to poke through his mangy fur. He stared at us for several seconds before dipping his muzzle to the water and drinking, huge pink tongue lapping up the frog spit. His tail swayed like a charmed cobra. After satisfying his thirst he looked at us again, and—I swear—winked. He left the same way he came.

"Lion," said the guard. What else could he say?

Neither of us moved for a minute. We heard screams from the other rooms. People ran through the courtyard in every direction, hollering in foreign languages. A small girl in a dress printed with giant sunflowers stood alone beneath the colonnade, hands covering her ears, eyes clenched shut.

They closed the museum for the remainder of the afternoon and all of us witnesses had to answer questions for hours—the police, the Park Service rangers, the television and newspaper reporters. I was interviewed on camera and then stood to the side, listening to the other accounts. A group of schoolchildren and chaperones from Buffalo had seen the lion walk out the museum's front door, search the sky like a farmer hoping for rain clouds, and walk slowly east. A bicycle courier spotted the lion on Park Avenue and promptly pedaled into a sewer grate, flipping over the handlebars and smashing his head against the curb. He spoke to the reporters while a paramedic wrapped gauze bandages around his forehead. After Park Avenue the lion seemed to disappear. A special police unit had scoured the surrounding blocks and found nothing. New Yorkers were being advised to stay indoors until further notice, advice that nobody took.

After all the interviews were over, the guard found me sitting on the bench by the frog fountain. "That was something," he said. "I need a beer. You want to get a beer somewhere?"

"I do," I said. "I really do."

We went to the Madison Pub, a dark old speakeasy where the gold-lettered names of long-dead regulars scrolled down the walls. We didn't say much during the first beer, didn't even exchange names until the food came.

"Louis Butchko," I said, repeating the name to help me remember it. My father had taught me that trick.

"Mm." He was chewing on a well-done cheeseburger. "Most people call me Butchko."

"He winked at us. Did you notice that? The lion, he winked."

"Hm?"

"I'm telling you, I saw him wink. He looked right at us and winked."

"Maybe. I didn't see it. One thing's for sure," he said, licking his lips, "they didn't mention lions when I applied for the job. Mostly they're afraid of people touching the paintings."

"He winked."

"I thought maybe a lunatic splashing yellow paint on the Titians, something like that, but lions? I ought to get, what do they call it, danger pay? Hazard pay?"

The bartender, an old Cypriot with dyed-black hair who had worked in the Pub since my father first took me there as a child, rubbed down the zinc bartop with a rag and a spray bottle. He whistled a tune that I could not place, a famous melody. It was maddening, the simple, evasive music.

"How long have you been here?" I asked Butchko.

"New York? Nine months. Down on Delancey."

"I like that neighborhood. You mind if I ask what you're paying?"

He took the pickle off his bun and offered it to me. It was a good pickle. "One-fifty."

"One-fifty? What does that mean?"

"One hundred and fifty dollars. A month."

I stared at him, waiting for an explanation.

"Come over and see the place sometime. I got a great deal. I met the superintendent and we worked it out. You know, New York is very expensive."

"Yes," I said.

"I didn't really have the money to move here, but it's one of the requirements. As a title holder."

"What title?" I examined his scrawny neck, his small white hands. "You're not a boxer?"

"Nope." He smiled, bits of blackened beef on his lips, in his teeth. "Nothing like that."

"You're going to make me guess? You're Anastasia, daughter of the czar?"

"It's something I kind of have to keep a low profile about. No publicity."

I sighed and waited.

"All right," he said, "all right. But you can't go around telling people. It's part of the deal, I have to keep it under-cover. I'm the Lover," he said, beaming a little in spite of himself.

"Okay," I said. "Whose lover?"

"No, *the* Lover. Capital *L*."

"Right," I said, finishing my beer. The bartender, quarter-ing limes, kept whistling his one song. "You're a porn star."

"No," he said, offended. "Nothing like that." He looked around the shadowy barroom, making sure nobody was within hearing distance. "The Lover of the East Coast. I'm the Greatest Lover on the East Coast. Not counting Florida, they're independent."

I smiled at him happily. The great thing about New York, no matter how insane you are, the next man over is bound to be twice as bad.

"What is there," I asked him, "a tournament?"

"It's not something you compete for," said Butchko. "It's more like the poet laureate. The last guy, Gregory Santos, he lives up in the Bronx, near Mosholu Parkway. Really nice guy. He took me out for drinks when I got the title, told me how to handle certain situations. He said it would change my whole life. The pressure is—I mean, women have *expectations* now. It's like being the New York Yankees."

I was pondering that for a while. The New York Yankees? No other customers remained in the bar, just the two of us and the bartender whistling. I imagined the Cypriot coming to work on the subway, head buried in the newspaper, while a small black-eyed girl sitting next to him whistled notes she heard at breakfast from her father's razor-nicked lips, notes her father heard the night before as he stood in a crowded elevator and watched the lighted floor numbers count down.

I concentrated on Butchko's sallow face, the purple blooms below his eyes. Studying a face will keep things quiet for a while. I tried to imagine that this was the man millions of East Coast women fantasized about while doodling in the margins of crossword puzzles. I tried to imagine him mounting bliss-faced seducees from the northern tip of Maine to Georgia, whispering in their ears, making them go all epileptic, their skin stretched so tight over rioting nerves that one touch in the right place would send them ricocheting around the room like an unknotted balloon.

I could picture the rapturous women because I had read about them in novels, had seen them in movies, but I had never held one in my arms. I had not touched a naked breast since the day my mother weaned me. The only contact I had with women was incidental: the brush of a supermarket clerk's fingers as she handed me my change, or an old lady tapping my shoulder, asking me to move aside so she could step off the bus. Like my beloved Saint Francis, I was a virgin.

"So what happened," I asked Butchko, "your high school girlfriend said you were the greatest?" I was trying to figure the origins of his fantasy.

He seemed mystified by the question. "Well, yeah."

There was something appealing about him. His delusions had originality, at least. All the other New York immigrants think they're the greatest actor, artist, writer, whatever—it was nice to meet the greatest lover.

The whistling Cypriot would never quit. Verse chorus verse chorus verse. If there was a bridge, the man didn't know it. I dug my knuckles into the corners of my eye sockets and breathed deeply.

"Mackenzie? You okay?"

"This *song*," I whispered. "What is this song he's whistling?"

" 'Paper Moon,' " said Butchko. He sang the chorus with the whistling as his accompanist. Butchko's voice was gorgeous, a pitch-perfect tenor, and for a moment I believed everything, all of it, the cities, towns, and countrysides full of quivering women sloshing about their bathtubs, moaning his name, *Butchko, Butchko,* wetting a thousand tiled floors in their delirium.

"Lion," he said, plowing the ketchup on his plate with the tines of his fork. "My first lion."

. . .

As soon as I got home I began preparing the house for my father, transferring six steaks from the freezer to the refrigerator, vacuuming the carpet in the master bedroom, stacking the logs and kindling in the library's fireplace, arranging the ivory chess pieces in their proper formations. I knew that he would have heard about the lion, that he would be on a plane crossing the Atlantic. We lived in a turn-of-the-century brownstone, the facade adorned with wine-grape clusters and leering satyrs. My room was on the top floor, beneath a skylight of pebbled glass. After the house was made ready for its master, I locked myself in my bedroom and turned off the lights.

Not counting the skylight there was only one window in my room, small and round as a porthole, facing south. Next to this window, mounted on a tripod, stood a brass telescope that my father had given me for my twelfth birthday. The telescope had belonged to the Confederate general Jubal Early; his monogram was stamped into the brass below the eyepiece. Humbled telescope: once used to track Union troop movements in the Shenandoah Valley, now spying on the *bento*-box apartments of New Yorkers. A red-haired woman watching television with a thermometer in her mouth; four young girls sitting cross-legged on the living room rug, folding origami cranes; an old man, bare-chested, arms folded on the windowsill, looking over me to Harlem; two women, one old, one young, slow dancing in the kitchen; a small boy with a bowl haircut, wearing Superman pajamas, lying in bed reading a book.

I peered into the building's other windows to make sure everyone was safe. That was my nightly ritual—I was a responsible voyeur. Sometimes I half-hoped to see smoke pouring from a toaster oven so that I could call the fire department and watch the snorkel truck raise its boom to the redhead's window, watch the fireman pluck her from danger. Even in my fantasies I wasn't the hero.

I capped the telescope's lens and eyepiece, undressed, climbed into bed. It was a marvelous bed, with four tall cedarwood posts and handwoven mosquito netting from the Ivory Coast. There weren't many mosquitoes in the brownstone, but I loved how the netting swayed in the air conditioner's breeze, pale lungs inhaling and exhaling.

In the strange space between sleeping and waking I imagined myself lionized. I paced the avenues, mane dreadlocked by city dirt. I met my stone brothers on the Public Library's steps; I sat with them and watched the beat cop pass, orange poncho clad, walkie-talkie chattering on his hip. I went underground, below the sidewalks, prowled the subway tunnels. The big-bellied rats fled when they smelled my hide. I curled up beside a soliloquizing madman, a filthy bundle of piss-damp rags, once a babe in a cradle, a shiny possibility. I licked the dirt from his face; he buried his head in my mane.

Soon he slept, and it was the first good sleep he'd had in years.

. . .

Rain pounded the pebbled glass of my skylight, the hoof-steps of a cavalry brigade heard from a great distance. It was almost dawn. The house was less empty than it had been. I pulled on a pair of green plaid pajamas, walked downstairs and knocked on the door of the master bedroom.

"Come in," called my father.

I opened the door. He sat cross-legged on the floor, the parts of his rifle disassembled, gleaming and oiled, on a spotted towel thrown over his steamer trunk. He wore his undershirt and a grass-stained pair of khakis; wire-framed glasses; a black steel wristwatch with a nonreflective face, the gift of a Ugandan general.

If you are sitting in your home, late at night, alone, strange noises echoing down the hallways, disturbing your mind, and if you look out across the street, look through the window of a stranger's apartment, the apartment lit only by the television's static, and the stranger's room glows a cool and eerie blue—that was the exact color of my father's eyes.

He wiped his hands clean on a corner of the towel, stood up, walked over and clasped my shoulders, kissed me on the forehead. "You look thin."

"I was sick for a while. I'm okay."

"You're eating?" He watched me carefully. I was never able to lie to my father. I mean, I was able to lie to him but I never got away with it.

"I forget sometimes." That was the truth. On bad days

the idea of eating seemed somehow ridiculous, or indulgent.

He walked to his desk, a rolltop of luminous mahogany that supposedly belonged to Stonewall Jackson. Hanging on the wall above the desk were four masks—carved wood embellished with feathers and shredded raffia—that my father had bought in Mali. Each represented a figure from the old Bambaran saying: "What is a crow but a dove dipped in pitch? And what is a man but a dog cursed with words?"

My father pulled a sheaf of fax papers from his desktop and looked through them. "I saw your name in here. You were one of the witnesses?"

"He winked at me."

My father continued reading through the papers, holding them at arm's length because his prescription was too weak and he never bothered to get reexamined. Being farsighted had no effect on his aim, though. I remember reading a profile of my father in a glossy hunting magazine; accompanying the article was a photograph of a silver dollar that had been neatly doughnuted by a high-caliber bullet. The caption below the picture read: *Shot by Mac-Gregor Bonner at 400 Yards in the Transvaal (prone position).* My father had bet a drunk Johannesburg socialite one thousand dollars that he could make the shot; when the woman paid up she told him, "I hope I never make you angry, Bonner."

My father read through the fax papers and I said again, "He winked at me. The lion. He was staring right at me and then he winked and then he walked away."

My father removed his glasses and hung them, by one

stem, from the neck of his undershirt. He pinched the bridge of his nose for a moment and then laughed.

"All mammals blink, Mackenzie. It keeps the eyeballs from drying out."

"Wink, not blink. He winked at me."

A sad smile lingered on his face as he regarded me. It was the Smile for Mackenzie, the expression he reserved for me alone. This is what you need to know about my father: He was a man who made a living killing animals, though he adored animals and disdained men. But I was his love's son and that gave me immunity from disdain, immunity from the cool hunter's stare he aimed at everyone else. His turn in this world was far from gentle, but he was gentle with me.

· · ·

Nobody saw the lion for the next five days. Wildlife experts on television speculated on his disappearance and proposed various possibilities for his whereabouts, but nobody knew anything. My father met with the chief of police and the mayor to coordinate the hunt. He inspected the sites where the lion had been seen and carefully studied all the eyewitness reports. In the terse interviews he gave to carefully chosen members of the press, he urged the public to remain cautious. He believed that the lion was still on the island of Manhattan.

Six days after I first saw the lion, on a humid afternoon—the kind where every surface is wet to the touch, as if the city itself were sweating—Butchko called and invited me to come over. I had forgotten that I gave him my number, and at first I was reluctant to go all the way downtown in the miserable August heat. But I had nothing better to do and I was curious to get a look at his one-hundred-and-fifty-dollar apartment.

I met him on the stoop steps of his building. Before I could speak he raised a finger to his lips and motioned me to sit beside him. The hysterical dialogue of a Mexican *telenovela* spilled from the open window of the first-floor apartment. I let the language wash over me, the rolling *r*'s, the sentences that all seemed to rhyme. Every few minutes I'd recognize a word and nod. *Loco! Cerveza! Gato!*

"*Te quiero,*" said Butchko, practicing the accent during a commercial break. "*Te quiero, te quiero, te quiero.*"

"You speak Spanish?"

"I'm learning. Gregory Santos said bilinguality is one of the seven steps to the full-out shudders."

Bilinguality? "What's the full-out—"

The soap opera came on again and Butchko hushed me. We listened to a hoarse-voiced man calm a distraught woman. A swell of violins and cellos seemed to signal their reconciliation and I imagined the kiss, the woman's eyes closed, tears of happiness rolling down her face as the darkly handsome man wrapped her in his arms. Butchko nodded solemnly.

When the show ended he led me into the brownstone and up a poorly lit staircase, pointing out various obstacles to avoid: a dogshit footprint, a toy car, broken glass. At the top of the last flight of stairs he pushed open a graffiti-tagged door and led me onto the tarpapered roof. A water tower squatted on steel legs alongside a shingled pigeon coop.

"You hang out up here?" I asked.

"This is home," he said, closing the door behind me and securing it with a combination lock. "Look," he said, pointing. "That's a pigeon coop."

"I know it's a pigeon coop."

"Ask me why it has two doors."

The coop was windowless and low-slung, narrow and long, hammered together of gray weathered boards. Splits in the wood had been stuffed with pink fiberglass insulation. A yellow door hung crooked in its frame on one end; I circled around the coop and found an equally crooked red door on the opposite end.

"Why does it have two doors?"

"Because if it had four doors it would be a pigeon sedan."

He was so happy with the joke his face turned bright red. He opened up his mouth and shined his big white Pennsylvania teeth at me. "Oh, Mackenzie. You walked right into that one."

I opened the red door and stepped inside. There were no pigeon cubbies, just a green sleeping bag, patched in places with electrical tape, unrolled on the bare wood flooring; a space heater, unplugged for the summer; a clock radio playing the Beatles; a blue milk crate stacked with paperbacks; an electric water-boiler; and a pyramid of instant ramen noodles in Styrofoam cups. The wires ran into a surge protector connected to a thick yellow extension cord that snaked down a neatly bored hole in the floor.

"The super sets me up with electric," said Butchko, standing in the doorway behind me. We had to stoop to fit below the steeply canted ceiling. "Pretty good deal, I think."

"Don't you get cold up here?" Even with the space heater at full blast, the coop could not be good shelter in the depths of winter.

Butchko shrugged. "I don't sleep here most nights, you know?"

I picked a paperback off the top of the pile. *The Selected Poetry of Robert Browning.* I read a few lines then returned the book to its brothers. "There's a toilet somewhere?"

"Down in the basement. And a shower, too. If I need to pee I just go off the roof, see how far I can get. Here, look at this." He ushered me out of the converted coop to the edge of the roof. We leaned against the parapet and looked at the brick wall of the building opposite us. "See the fire escape? I hit it the other day. What do you think, twenty feet across?"

With my eyes I followed the ladders and landings of the fire escape down to the alley below, deserted save for a blue Dumpster overflowing with trash.

"It's just rats down there anyway," said Butchko. "They don't mind a little pee. Or maybe they do, but screw 'em, they're rats. And then, here, this is the best part. Come over here."

In the cool shadow of the water tower he grabbed a canteen off the tarpaper and began climbing the steel rungs welded onto one of the tower's legs. I walked back into the sunlight to watch his ascent. At the upper lip of the tower he turned and waved to me, thirty feet below, before pulling himself over the edge and disappearing from view. A minute later he started climbing down. He jumped with five feet to go and hit his landing perfectly.

"Here," he said, offering me the canteen. I drank cold water.

"There's a tap up there for the inspectors. They come twice a year and check things out, make sure there's no bacteria or whatnot floating around."

I handed him back the canteen and watched him drink, watched his heavy Adam's apple bob in his throat.

"Are you ever going to tell me what the full-out shudders are?"

Butchko grinned. "Come on, Mackenzie, you've been there."

"Where?"

He capped the canteen and laid it down in the shade of the tower. "The shudders are reality," he said, and by the way he said it I knew he was quoting. "The shudders are the no-lie reality. Listen, women are very different from men."

"Oh! Ah!"

"Well, okay, it sounds obvious, but it's important. For a man, sex is simple. He gets in and he gets off. But it's not automatic for a woman."

It wasn't automatic for me either, but I kept my mouth shut.

"The thing is, women are more sensitive than men. They don't want to hurt our feelings."

"Ha," I countered.

"In general," he said. "So they act, sometimes. They pretend. Now, for me, given my circumstances, it's very important that I know exactly what works and what doesn't. And I can't rely on what she's saying, or the groaning, the moaning, the breathing, none of that. Arching the back, curling the foot, biting the lip—none of that is a sure thing. Only the shudders. There's no faking the full-out shudders. You see those thighs start to quiver, I mean *quiver*, you know you found the pearl. Oysters and pearls, Mackenzie. Everybody knows where the oyster is—finding the pearl is what makes a good lover."

I stared at the water tower looming above us. The kid was a genuine lunatic, but I liked him.

"I'll tell you the first thing I learned, living in the city," said Butchko. "Puerto Rican women are excellent lovers."

"All of them?"

"Yes," he said. "All of them."

• • •

I smoked Lucky Strikes on the rooftop and talked with Butchko about women and lions until he told me he had to get ready for his date. Twenty minutes later I was riding the First Avenue bus uptown. "Air conditioner's broken," the driver told me before I stepped on. "There's another bus right behind me." He said the same thing to everyone, and everyone besides me grunted and waited for the next bus, but I paid the fare and sat in the back row. My decision displeased the driver. I think he wanted to drive his hot empty bus at high speeds, slamming on the brakes at red lights with no passengers to complain. I wouldn't have said a word. He could have cruised up the avenue at ninety miles per hour, swerving around the potholes; it didn't matter to me. I was easy.

When we passed under the Queensboro Bridge I saw the

lion. I shouted, a wordless shout, and the driver looked at me in his mirror and hit the brakes, as simple as that, as if he were used to riders shouting when they wanted to get off. I shoved through the heavy double doors at the rear of the bus and ran back to the bridge, under the shadowy barrel vault.

It could be that I read too much in a wink, and I wouldn't have been the first, but it seemed to me that the lion knew who I was. I believed that. I believed that the lion had a message for me, that the lion had come Lord knows how many miles in search of me, had evaded countless hunters in order to deliver his intelligence. Now he was here and my father had been hired to kill him. The lion would never make it back to Africa.

He waited for me on the sidewalk below the bridge. Flies crawled in the tangles of his mane. He watched me with yellow eyes. His hide sagged over his bones; the sore on his shoulder was inflamed, graveled with white pustules. His belly was distended, bloated from hunger. I thought of how far he was from home, how many thousands of miles he had traveled, so far from the zebras and wildebeests, the giraffes and antelopes of his native land, his nourishment. Here there were only people to eat. I could not imagine this lion stooping to devour the neighborhood mutts or the blinkered carriage-horses.

I wondered how long it would take him to gobble me down, and how much it would hurt, the long white teeth, the massive jaws, how long, and would he strip me to the wet bone or leave some meat for the pigeons to peck at, would he spit out my knuckles and watch them roll like

gambler's dice, would he look up from my carcass, his muzzle painted red, watch the taxis race by like stray gazelles
frantic for their herd?

"Speak to me," I pleaded, hungry for revelation. "Speak
to me."

If you have ever stood near a lion, you understand humil-
ity. Nothing that lives is more beautiful. A four-hundred-
pound lion can run down a thoroughbred, can tear through
steel railroad car doors with his claws, can hump his mate
eighty times in one day.

The lion rose to all fours and walked closer, until his whiskers were nearly brushing against my shirt. I closed my eyes
and waited. The carnivorous stink of him, the low purr of his
breathing, the mighty engine of him—I was ready. I got
down on my knees on the sidewalk, below the Queensboro
Bridge, and the lion's breath was hot as steam in my ear.

When I opened my eyes the lion was gone and I was shiv-
ering in the August heat. I hailed a taxi and directed the tur-
baned driver to the Frick Museum, but when I got there the
front doors of the old robber baron's mansion were bolted
shut. It was Monday, I remembered. The museum was
closed. That's why Butchko was home. It was the worst
possible time to be Monday, and I imagined that all days
would now be Monday, that we would suffer through
months of Mondays, that the office workers would rise day
after day and never come closer to the weekend, they would
check the newspaper each morning and groan, and the
churchgoers would find themselves, perpetually, a day too
late for the Sabbath.

I needed Bellini's Francis. I needed to stand with the virgin saint and experience the ecstasy, to feel the rapture driven through my palms, my feet. I needed to understand the language of animals, the words of the beasts, because when the lion whispered in my ear it sounded like nothing but the breath of a big cat. I needed translation.

I walked all the way home. The house was empty, every clock ticking solemnly until, in the space of a terrifying second, they yodeled the hour in unison. Whenever my father was in Africa I would quit winding the clocks; in every room their dead hands would mark the minute the pendulum stopped swinging. He always synchronized them the day he came home.

In my bedroom I uncapped the telescope's lens and eyepiece and studied the apartments across the street. The old man leaned against his windowsill, gazing toward Harlem. The redhead one floor below him seemed healthier; she lay belly-down on her carpeted floor, propped on her elbows, chewing a pencil, still working on Saturday's crossword. Behind her, on the television, Marlon Brando smooched Eva Marie Saint. The redhead never turned the TV off: not when she was away at work, not when she was sleeping. I understood—voices comforted her, even strangers' voices.

The redhead finished her crossword and began checking her answers against the solution in Monday's paper. The television behind her flashed an urgent graphic: Breaking News. A reporter wearing a safari hat and sunglasses began speaking into his microphone, gesturing to the crowd surrounding him. I tried to read his lips. Bored of the game, I was about to swing the telescope away when I saw the lion, *my* lion, star-ing into the camera. He sat by a fountain, a great round foun-tain with a winged angel standing above the waters.

I ran. Down the stairs, out the door, west on Eighty-fourth Street, dodging the street traffic, dashing across the avenues, York First Second Third Lexington Park Madison and Fifth, into Central Park, panting, sweat pouring into my eyes. All the way to Bethesda Fountain, at least a mile, far-ther than I had run in years. When I got there the crowd bulged way back to the band shell, hundreds of yards from the fountain. A man with a pushcart sold Italian ices and so-das. A news helicopter circled above us.

I shoved and sidled my way to the front lines, ignoring the dirty looks, the muttered heys, watchits, and yos. Blue police sawhorses barricaded the way, a cop stationed every ten feet. Two curving stone staircases flanked by balustrades swept down to the terrace. The lion sat patiently by the angel fountain. Behind him was the stagnant pond where paddle-boating tourists typically photographed the bushes and col-lided with each other and cursed in every language known to man. They had all been evacuated. I saw my father, halfway down the steps, on one knee, holding his rifle. Two Park Ser-vice rangers stood next to him, high-powered dart guns aimed at the lion. Police sharpshooters ringed the terrace.

At the back of the crowd people yelled and whistled and laughed, but up close, in view of the lion, there was cathedral silence. My father gave the order and the rangers pulled their triggers. Darts fly far slower than bullets; I could trace their black flight from gun barrels to lion's shoulder.

The lion roared. His jaws swung open and he roared. All the birds sitting in the trees burst from their branches and squawked skyward, a panicked flight of pigeons and sparrows. Everyone leaning against the barricades fell back, the entire crowd retreating a step as instincts commanded *run, run, run!* A lion's roar can be heard for five miles in the emptiness of the savanna. Even in Manhattan his protest echoed above the constant squall of car alarms and ambulance sirens, above the whistles of traffic cops and the low rumble of subway trains. I imagine that sunbathers in the Sheep Meadow heard the roar, and tourists in Strawberry Fields; that bicyclists squeezed their hand brakes and stood on their pedals, squinted through their sunglasses in the direction of the noise; that old men, piloting their remote-controlled miniature schooners across the algae-filmed water of the Boat Pond, looked west, leaving their ships to drift; that dogwalkers watched their charges go rigid, prick up their ears, then bark madly, until all the dogs in the borough were howling; that every domestic cat sitting on a windowsill stared heartlessly toward the park and licked its paws clean.

The lion stood unsteadily, blinking up at the sun. He began to walk, headed for the staircase, but stumbled after a few paces. Everyone in the crowd inhaled at the same moment. My father gave another command and two more darts pierced the lion's hide, releasing their tranquilizers. The rangers cradled their guns in their arms and waited; four darts were enough to put a rhino to sleep.

The lion charged. He reached the steps so quickly that

none of the sharpshooters had time to react; he bounded up the broad stone stairs, white fangs bared, while the rangers fumbled with their guns and the cops standing near me said "Jesus Christ" and backed into the sawhorses and mothers in the crowd covered their children's eyes.

In mid-leap the lion seemed to crash into an invisible wall; he twisted in the air and landed heavily on his side, front paws two steps above his hind paws. The rifle shot sounded as loud and final as a vault door slamming shut. My father ejected the spent shell and it glittered in the air before bouncing off the balustrade and into the vegetation below.

I ducked under the sawhorse, evading the dazed policemen, and ran down the stairs. My father saw me coming and shouted my name, but I was past him before he could stop me. I knelt down beside the lion and held his furred skull in my palms, my forearms buried in his dirty mane. He seemed smaller now, shrunken. The blood puddling beneath him began to drip down the steps.

"Tell me," I begged him, looking into his yellow eyes. My father was coming for me. I lowered my head so that my right ear rested against the lion's damp muzzle. "Tell me."

A series of violent spasms ran down the length of his outstretched body. Each breath exited his lungs with an unnerving whistle. His jaws slowly parted. I closed my eyes and waited. He licked my face with his mighty tongue until my father collared me and dragged me aside. I did not watch the mercy shot.

. . .

Hours later, when I stood in the shower and let the hot water beat down on me, I picked three blue splinters from my palms. It took me a while to figure out that they came from gripping the police sawhorse by Bethesda Fountain. After the shower I toweled myself dry, pulled on my pajamas, climbed the stairs to my bedroom, locked the door behind me, and switched off the lights. A pale moon shone weakly through the pebbled glass. I tried to remember how many miles away she was, how many cold miles of sky I would need to climb. It seemed impossible to me that men had ever walked there, had ever cavorted in her loose gravity.

When I was young I had known the number, known her distance to the mile. I had known her diameter, her weight in metric tons, the names of her major craters, the precise duration of her rotation around the earth. I forgot everything.

I uncapped General Early's telescope and scanned the apartments opposite. Whatever the old man was looking for in Harlem, he had quit for the night—the lamps were all out and the shades drawn. The little boy was awake. He sat beneath his sheets with a flashlight—a one-boy tent—furtively reading when he was supposed to be sleeping.

I checked the other rooms in my customary search for fire, and this night I found it. Not in the boy's apartment but one flight down, candles burning atop the stereo speakers and bookshelves, the coffee table and turned-off television, the windowsill and mantel. The redhead, naked, straddled a man on her sofa, her hands resting on his narrow shoulders. In the candlelight her flanks were mapped with copper trails of sweat. She rose and fell like a buoy in the sea, bobbing with the waves. Before I turned away, to give them their privacy, the woman flung her head back and stiffened for an instant, her hands falling from Butchko, her fingers spread wide. Her mouth opened but I'm sure no words came out, no words at all, nothing but ecstasy.

THE BAREFOOT GIRL IN CLOVER

1

When I was sixteen I stole a midnight blue '55 Eldorado convertible and drove to Hershey Park for the afternoon. I never intended to stop in Hershey—nobody flees New Jersey for Pennsylvania. The plan—*plan*! as if I had plotted the whole thing in advance—was two days to California, buying gasoline and potato chips with my father's credit card, never sleeping till I saw the Pacific glittering through the windshield. I chickened out. I had the balls to go, but I didn't have the balls to stay gone.

For seven hours, though, I ruled the road. The sharkish tailfins cut the air behind me; *London Calling* played on the tape deck, over and over; a Virgin Mary statuette swayed from the rearview mirror, her eyes downcast with modesty or dismay. I stole the Cadillac from a Catholic, a senior named Tommy Byrnes Jr. When Tommy had pulled into the parking lot that morning before classes, a crowd of boys gathered around the car, saying *Damn!* and *Whoa!* and *Hoo yeah!* It was a fearsome machine, its chrome grille shining like a mouthful of teeth. It looked like the bully of the freeways, eager to hunt down weaker cars and devour them.

I wanted it. I said, "Tommy, let me run it around the block one time."

He laughed uneasily. "You don't even have your license."

"I've got my learner's permit. You ride shotgun."

Even then, as a sophomore, I was the biggest kid in the school, second-team all-state at left tackle. I was getting handwritten letters from football coaches at Division One universities. People at Mahlus High treated me well. Still, Tommy didn't want me driving his father's car. He explained it to me in detail, the hell he would suffer if somebody got fingerprints on the paint job. A dented fender was certain death. If it was *his* car he'd be glad to let me gun it down the avenues, blasting the horn at every girl we passed, but there was no way, no possibility, that I could drive his father's Eldorado.

I smiled and nodded and held out my hand for the keys.

"Come on, Zabrocki," said Tommy, shaking his head, and "I can't, man," and "Look, it's not *mine*," and finally "Once around the block. Slowly."

That was the first car I ever sat in that felt as if it were built for someone my size. There was room to stretch my legs and the steering wheel wasn't jammed against my chest. The roof was down and I had miles of open air above my head.

Tommy got in and said, "You know how to drive stick, right?"

"Sure," I said, turning the key.

"The clutch, Zabrocki. Hit the clutch."

At the corner of Hudson and Blair, where we stopped for a red light, Tommy said, "You're ruining the gearbox."

"Maybe you should take over," I said, opening my door. Tommy nodded happily and got out of the car. Instead of standing I slammed my door and stepped on the gas. The engine roared but the car didn't move. Tommy stared at me.

"What are you doing?"

I finally remembered to shift into first and the Eldorado bolted across the intersection, under the red light. Tommy Byrnes Jr. stood motionless in the Blair Street crosswalk. I watched him dwindle away in the rearview mirror. I figured I'd cruise over to the diner for a triple fried-egg sandwich and be back at school before second period started, but after I'd driven six blocks I realized there would be no schooling for me that day. The Eldorado was freshly washed and waxed, the tank was full, my father's credit card—on loan for the express purpose of buying a new lawnmower that afternoon—was tucked into my jeans pocket, and the sun had already burned away the morning fog. It was May, the days were long, I had a biology test third period and I could never remember the difference between meiosis and mitosis.

I knew Tommy wouldn't call the cops. He'd expect me to return to school smirking, tossing him the keys and laughing at what a fool I'd made of him. He wouldn't want his father to find out that he'd lent the Eldorado to a kid with a learner's permit, so he'd walk back to the school parking lot and wait for me.

This story is making me sound like an asshole; I'm aware of that. I won't blame it on my youth. I knew exactly how miserable Tommy had to feel, I knew I was screwing him over, I knew all about it and I didn't care. It was a beautiful spring day; I was driving a convertible with *tailfins*; when I turned on the tape deck I heard Joe Strummer's guitar licks. There are days when you need to live in violation.

I picked up Route 202 outside of town and headed west. California lay that way, and though I had never thought much about California before, it seemed the natural destination for a young man with a stolen Eldorado. The secret to driving stick, I discovered, was always hitting the clutch. Hit the clutch when starting the car, when shifting gears, when signaling a turn. Simple. All I needed was a girl to stroke my thigh and navigate.

I stuck to the speed limit and winked at the pretty mothers who passed me in their station wagons. I found a pair of aviator sunglasses in the glove compartment. They were too small but I wore them anyway.

Paying the toll with the last coins in my pocket, I crossed the Delaware into Pennsylvania, stopping in New Hope to buy an ice-cream cone at Thomas Sweet's. They weren't happy that I charged it on the credit card, they told me there was a ten-dollar minimum, blah blah blah, but I was already holding the cone and licking it. I stood by the Eldorado eating my ice cream, watching the tourists scour the antiques shops.

I gobbled down the rest of the cone and set off for California. After an hour on the road I decided I was still famished, so I drove through the small town of North Wales in search of a hamburger joint. A very small town—people stared at me as I rolled by, as if I were an evil cowboy clopping down Main Street on my black horse. I passed a hardware store and a ninety-nine-cent store and a barbershop and a church and then mile after mile of green farm fields. I don't know what they were growing—I'm a townie; if it's not wheat or corn, I'm lost—but there was a lot of it and it went on forever. I saw a girl in denim shorts and a paint-splattered T-shirt bicycling on the side of the road and I pulled over in front of her. She pedaled up to my door, rested one bare foot on the asphalt, and looked down at me in my Cadillac cockpit. Her bicycle was old-fashioned, with a wicker basket in front adorned with a yellow plastic sunflower.

"I'm looking for Wales," I told her. She didn't say anything so I added, "There's nothing to eat in North Wales."

"There is no Wales," she said, her voice surprisingly husky. She was older than I had first thought, around my age, with a freckled complexion, brown eyes, and dirty blond hair that looked as if it had been hacked at with a machete. She stared at my hands resting on the steering wheel and said, "What do you play, O-line?"

The Pennsylvania kids I knew from football camp were bred tough. As a rule, they weren't as athletic as the kids from California or Florida, they weren't as well coached as the kids from Texas, but when they played they treated their bodies like rental cars. One time, when a bunch of us were sitting around the lake after dinner, a Stroudsburg boy asked me if I wanted to play stone with them. Sure, I said. How do you play? All the Pennsylvania kids jumped up and pelted me with pebbles. I chased after them but they were wide receivers and safeties and they laughed and catcalled as I lumbered in hopeless pursuit.

"O-line," I told the barefoot girl. "What happened to Wales?"

"Nothing happened to it," she said. "There never was one."

That seemed strange to me, a town called North Wales with no Wales below it, but I was deep in the boondocks and I didn't want to start debating with the natives.

"Is there somewhere around here to get a burger?"

She grinned at me. Her front teeth were chipped. "We're still in America, big man. We've got Burger King and everything."

"Which way is that?"

"Onion rings sound good," she said. "Give me a ride and I'll direct."

She wheeled her bicycle off the shoulder and dumped it into the green stalks, the growing things. I should have asked her what they were, but I wasn't thinking about crops. I was watching her frayed denim shorts; her sun-burned arms, legs, and nose; her white throat. My navigator.

She got in and pointed. "Straight on."

I stalled the car and the girl said, "Put that huge foot of yours on the clutch."

"I know," I said, remembering the good times when it was just me and the machine zooming along in peace. I finally got the car moving again. "I'm Leon," I told her.

"I'm Maureen. Most people call me Reen."

"Reen? What do the other people call you?"

She frowned. "Maureen."

I turned up the volume and Maureen sang along, kicking her dirty bare feet up on the dashboard. She twitched her toes to the beat. Her nails were painted silver. "Whose car?" she asked.

"My dad's."

"I thought maybe you stole it. I thought we could be outlaws." She made two pistols with her hands and fired away through the windshield. "Bonnie and Clyde."

"My dad doesn't know I took it," I said, wishing I'd told her the truth. I really was an outlaw but I wasn't getting any credit.

"My mom doesn't know I cut school." She flicked the hem of the Virgin Mary's robe and watched the statuette dance back and forth. "I'm Catholic, too."

So I fell in love right then, Mick Jones wailing over the speakers, the Virgin Mary swaying, Maureen's dirty feet on the dashboard. It wasn't her looks, though I thought she was lovely. It was her fearlessness. She was absolutely unafraid of me. The girls at Mahlus High tended to treat me like Lenny from *Of Mice and Men*; they thought if I got too excited I might pet them real hard and snap their necks. But Maureen was at ease sitting next to me. We glided through the farmland and I forgot about my hunger; I forgot about Tommy Byrnes Jr. and his father, who must be calling the police by now; I forgot about the biology test and the Golgi apparati. There are a few moments in your life when you are truly and completely happy, and you remember to give thanks. Even as it happens you are nostalgic for the moment, you are tucking it away in your scrapbook. I was sixteen years old and already second-team All–New Jersey at left tackle; I was driving a midnight blue Cadillac Eldorado to

California; my navigator knew the lyrics to The Clash songs and painted her toenails silver. I was winning.

At the Burger King drive-thru we bought Whoppers and fries and onion rings and milkshakes, one vanilla, one strawberry. The girl at the window was pretty in a mean way, with skinny lips and dark-blue eye shadow. She glared at me when I offered the credit card and shook her head.

"Cash only. No school today, Reen?"

"No school this year, Lannie?"

"This your new boyfriend? Where'd you get the car, boyfriend?"

I had opened the glove compartment and was searching for stray coins or bills. Maureen's legs, bare below the white threads of frayed denim, smelled of soap and sweat and grass. One knee was skinned and starting to scab over. I looked up into her face and she looked back, arching one eyebrow expertly.

"What's the story, Reen, you got a new boyfriend for every day of the week?"

Maureen ran a hand back and forth over my flattop and smiled at the girl. "You put too much face on your makeup, Lannie."

Lannie's skinny lips curled back from her teeth as she leaned through the window. "You've got a real slut in your car, rich boy. I guess she already sucked up all your cash."

Maureen pulled a ten-dollar bill from her pocket and handed it to me. I sat up in my seat, gave Lannie the money, and took back the change and the paper bags of food. "Thank you for choosing Burger King," she told me, sliding the window shut.

We continued west, chewing on our burgers meditatively. When it became clear that Maureen wasn't going to explain anything, I said, "You and Lannie like the same guy or something?"

"She's my cousin. She's not so bad. This place drives you crazy after a while." She sighed and twirled an onion ring around her index finger.

"I'm heading to California," I told her. "You can come, if you want."

"Yeah," she said. "Why not?"

"I'll buy dinner on my credit card."

After we finished eating Maureen burped delicately into the back of her hand and said, "Now we need dessert. You like chocolate?"

During wrestling season I competed as a heavyweight, which meant that for matches and tournaments I needed to weigh in at less than 275 pounds. That fall I'd gotten close to 300, and when winter came I was dieting for the first time in my life, jogging around the school's steamy indoor pool in a rubber suit, and spitting into a cup during class, which my teammates assured me was good for at least six ounces a day. One of the things I gave up that winter was chocolate, and some nights I dreamed that I swam through a lake of melted chocolate, breathing chocolate, swallowing peanut-butter fishes when I could catch them.

"I like chocolate," I told her.

"Take a left at the stoplight," she said.

"Ooh, *stoplight*."

"Yeah," she said. "Sometimes we just sit here and watch it change colors. *Left*, Leon. Your other left."

We picked up Route 422 and sped along, the needle pointing directly at fifty-five. I ended up telling her the truth about the car and she thought I ought to call Tommy Byrnes Jr. and tell him everything was okay, but that I shouldn't call him until we got our chocolate, and that would take a while. I told her about my family: my baby brother Ollie who was two years old; my father who had made a fortune selling life insurance on the Jersey Shore; my mother who taught at the school for the deaf in Elizabeth, an hour commute each way, and how much those kids loved her, and how kind they were, and how strange it was that deaf kids were so much nicer than kids with ears that worked.

Maureen told me that her parents got married in Las Vegas and they were divorced six months after she was born. Her father still lived in Vegas; he was one of the highest-paid blackjack dealers in town; he drove a Porsche with a license plate that read 214ME. Maureen was going to move there after high school and he would teach her the tricks of the trade. She could already shuffle like a pro. Her mother had made a big mistake by remarrying and losing her alimony—the stepdad was a creep and hadn't held a real job in three years. Maureen had a little sister named Emily who was four and would be perfect for Ollie.

Each time the Clash tape ended I would flip it to the other side. We never got sick of it. I was getting hungry again, but I didn't want Maureen to think my stomach ruled me, so I didn't say anything for eight minutes. When my patience finally ran out I asked, "So where is this chocolate store?"

She smiled and punched my arm. "We're getting there. Relax, big man. This is the good part."

The girl was right. If the car had been stocked with sausages I could have driven with her to the southern tip of Chile, listening to *London Calling* the whole way, phoning Tommy Byrnes Jr. from Cape Horn to apologize. "But Jesus Christ, Tommy, have you ever seen the Southern Cross?"

"Anyway," I said to Maureen, "they better not run out of chocolate before we get there."

"No," she said. "I don't think they will."

We left the farms behind and the road cut across a series of wooded hills. I was now able to shift gears with almost no grinding noises whatsoever, and I began showing off for Maureen, fading into the turns, downshifting on the steep slopes, waving to the truckers who zipped by in the opposite direction.

After we came around a sharp curve I began to smell something different in the air, a wonderful smell, familiar and strange at the same time. It was a smell that reminded me of before I was big, when I stood in the kitchen with my thumb in my mouth and watched mom open the oven and peer inside.

"Chocolate," I said. The hills smelled like solid chocolate.

"Chocolate," agreed Maureen. She laughed diabolically— *mwa-ha-ha! mwa-ha-ha!*—her head tilted back, exposing that wondrous white throat, laughing the laugh of a jinni who has just tricked a man out of his final wish. We passed under an arched sign: HERSHEY PARK—THE SWEETEST PLACE ON EARTH.

We parked the Eldorado in a giant lot that was nearly empty.

"This place is packed in the summer," she said. I thought it would be a good idea to put the top up, but neither of us could figure out how it worked. "It'll be safe," she said. "It's the sweetest place on earth."

We walked down Cocoa Avenue. The tops of the streetlights were shaped like Hershey's Kisses. Everything smelled like chocolate. We strolled through Hershey Gardens, where the tulips were blooming, and stopped for a snack at the Hotel Hershey. The doorman shook his head and told us, "No shoes, no service." He said it as if he were the first person to think of the line. I went in alone and bought three tuna-melt sandwiches, six hard-boiled eggs, two hot dogs, a one-pound chocolate bar, and two Styrofoam cups of milk, carried the food outside in a plastic bag bearing the Hershey's logo. Maureen and I sat down to eat on the hotel's patio but the doorman left his post to tell us that the patio was for guests only. The anger started pouring through me and it felt good; it felt pure. I stood and stared down into his blunt, sullen face, ready to squeeze his skull until snot popped out his nostrils, but Maureen grabbed my hand and led me to a bench near the Gardens, and we finally ate in peace. Or I ate and Maureen watched. She didn't seem disturbed by the quantities I consumed. She seemed to think it was normal.

After lunch we went to the amusement park and rode on a roller coaster, a Ferris wheel, and a carousel. We gave each other whiplash in the bumper cars and then Maureen said, "I ought to get home pretty soon. My sister gets scared when she's alone with mom too long."

The drive back east seemed faster. Maureen took a nap, her head resting on my shoulder. She talked in her sleep, excitedly, but the only words I could make out were, *No fair.* I turned the radio's volume down and when I looked at the road again I saw that we were about to slam into a refrigerator lying on its back. I swerved into the opposite lane and missed it by inches. One lone car followed me a ways back; I flashed my hazards as a warning for him. After my follower slowed and switched lanes, he blinked his headlights to thank me, and Maureen slept on. I felt beloved and loving, at peace with my fellows, a good man making his way through the world.

When we got back to North Wales I woke Maureen and she directed me to the spot where she had dumped her bicycle. She got out of the car and stepped lightly through the clover and long grass that grew between the pavement and the farm field. She found her bike lying in the green crops, lifted it upright, and walked it over to the driver's side door. I thought I should get out of the car to say good-bye but Maureen didn't let me; she bent down and kissed me on the mouth. A truck rumbled by, blowing its horn.

It was the first good kiss of my life. Her lips tasted like chocolate. When it was over she reached into her hip pocket and handed me a folded candy-bar wrapper. On the inside she had written her name and telephone number. She had drawn a pig's face, and from the pig's mouth a dialogue bubble with the words *Don't forget about me!*

"I won't," I said, and I wanted to say more but I was sixteen and dumb, and Maureen got onto her bicycle and pedaled away.

I drove back to New Jersey with the tape deck silent. I didn't want to listen to Joe and Mick if Maureen wasn't accompanying them on backing vocals. The whole ride to Mahlus was miserable. I wanted it to rain, I wanted the weather to match my mood, but the sun kept shining and I thought, some day, California.

When I got to the high school parking lot I expected to see cops waiting for me, but there was nothing but the usual beat-down faculty cars and snazzy senior cars. That was one problem with Mahlus High. The students didn't respect the teachers because the teachers were poor, and the teachers didn't respect the students because the students were rich.

I parked the Eldorado and walked over to the baseball diamond. I found Tommy in the outfield, shagging fly balls. He played baseball, basketball, and football, he wasn't much good at any of them, but he never missed a practice. He saw me coming and threw down his glove. I walked up to him, waiting for him to swing. I knew I deserved it but I also knew that if Tommy punched me I would have to punch him back, that once I started on him it would take the whole baseball team to tear me off, that Tommy would get hurt and I would be labeled a bully. He never swung. I handed him the keys and started to speak but Tommy turned away from me and walked off the field, leaving his mitt behind. A baseball hit the grass a few feet from me and I picked it up and threw it back to the batting cage, where the coach was hitting fungoes with an aluminum bat.

Maureen and Hershey Park seemed very far behind me,

very distant, as if they were another boy's memories, stolen with the Eldorado, returned now to their rightful owner. I sat in the grass and watched the baseballs fall from the blue sky into the outfielders' waiting gloves.

2

Fourteen years later I was at home by myself, watching a rental movie on the VCR, an old James Cagney gangster flick. Midway through came a few seconds of static and then two sweating black men, one of them on his knees giving the other a blow job. For almost a minute I stared at the screen, trying to figure out what all this had to do with bank heists, fedoras, Tommy guns. The man getting sucked off had the most amazing smile on his face—the gates of paradise were opened wide and he was marching through, saints by his side. I've never smiled like that, I said to myself; I never will smile like that. What am I doing with this life?

It's not what you're thinking. I didn't decide that what I really needed was a blow job from a black man. Maybe that's exactly what I need, maybe that's the cure for all that ails me, but that's not where my mind was going. I thought: this is *me*, this is how it goes, not one movie with logical plot progression but a wild medley of every genre: porno and screwball comedy and teen romance and horror. No cowboys, not yet, and no starships, but give it time.

I pushed the stop button and imagined the laughter of some bored prankster, rubbing his palms with glee as he hatched this scheme weeks or months before. Whoever he was, he knocked me for a loop. I sat on the sofa for an hour with the lights and television off, with no beer in my hand, with no sounds at all to disturb me except the occasional car passing on Rickover Street.

I had always expected to be famous. I figured I'd play professional football and there would be a room in Mahlus High devoted to my memorabilia; I would appear with my model wife in television commercials for the United Way; in the postgame interviews my quarterback would never forget to thank me for saving his ass. Things didn't work out. Senior year of college I broke my neck blocking on a halfback sweep; I was paralyzed for sixteen hours and the doctors thought it might be for life. The surgeons fused two vertebrae and a month later I was relearning how to walk.

My father sat with me in the hospital room day after day. One morning I started crying and could not stop. I told him how sorry I was, because I knew how much he loved watching me play. I told him that it felt like I had lost a fight, *the* fight, that I wasn't tough enough, and my father shook his head and said there never was a fight. It was just an accident. I said it *was* a fight and I lost. My father could not look at me. He watched the floor and repeated that it was just an accident, and even if it was a fight, there was no shame in losing a fight—everyone but Rocky Marciano did.

When graduation came I sat with the rest of my class in our black gowns and mortarboards. I had lost eighty pounds since the accident. My old shirts flopped around my shoulders, mocking me with the memory of when I was huge. When my name was called over the loudspeaker, I stood up and walked very deliberately to the platform, climbed the four steps—left foot, right foot, left foot, right foot—and accepted my diploma from the beaming university president. She stood on her tiptoes to kiss me on the forehead and everybody there—the seniors, their parents, the alumni, the faculty—stood up and cheered for a minute straight. *Le-on! Le-on! Le-on!*

At the end of that summer dad took me into his office and began teaching me the insurance business. It turned out I was made for it. People around Mahlus knew who I was, they remembered what had happened to me, and that was always good for starting conversations. "We were rooting for you," they would tell me. "We prayed for you."

After seven years my father decided I had figured the racket out. When he turned sixty he announced that he was sick to death of winter. He bought a house in Jupiter, Florida, and moved down there with my mother and little brother, leaving me to run the business, and I've done all right so far. I work hard. Some nights I go drinking with friends, other nights I stay home and watch the sitcoms or a rented movie.

On that night, the night of the Cagney/blow job prank, I couldn't get the porn actor's smile out of my mind. He was happiness. He was exactly where he wanted to be. Only two things ever made me that happy, football and women, but these days I'm not much of a football fan. I only loved the sport because I was good at it; I was made for the game. I'm too goddamn big for anything else.

Football couldn't make me happy anymore, so I thought about women. Ex-girlfriends, one-night stands, insurance brokers I knew from work, friends from college who had married and disappeared from my life, women I saw at the gym, my buddies' wives. I got them all partying in the same nightclub in my mind, and I looked at them from every angle—their smiles, their thighs, their ankles—and I listened to bits of conversation, snippets of dialogue I remembered from various encounters. They were all there, looking as good as they ever had, speaking their most memorable lines. And I was happy keeping them in that imagined nightclub. I didn't have any desire to yank them into my reality—the dark living room, the sofa, me.

A new girl walked into this party and I studied her face. She was familiar but I could not place her until my mind's camera panned down and recorded her paint-splattered T-shirt, her denim cutoffs, her bare and dirty feet.

After fourteen years Maureen's face had blurred and finally disappeared from memory. Now, though, in my empty living room, I could see her again perfectly: her brown eyes, her chipped front teeth, her home-cut dirty-blond hair.

In college I loved telling people about the stolen Eldorado. First, because it's a true story, and second, because it made it sound as if my adolescence were impossibly dramatic, as if my life would be made into a road movie starring a brooding teenager who flicks his cigarette butts into the gutter and wins fistfights started by big men with tattoos. Except I was the big man with tattoos and nobody wanted to film my life.

After remembering Maureen's face and how comfortable I had felt with her, how happy we had been for five hours, I wondered where she was and if she had already found her man. For some reason I doubted it; for some reason I was positive that she was sitting in the dark somewhere, alone, remembering faces.

The next morning, a Monday, I called my secretary and told her I would be in Pennsylvania for the day, scouting a few leads. I couldn't remember if Maureen had ever told me her last name. She had given me her number, she had written it on the back of a Hershey wrapper, but I had lost it years before. The first few weeks after we met I was too nervous to call, and then I got scared that she had already forgotten me, and then came junior year and a spectacular season and I grew cocky. If I could chance upon girls like her in a no-account town, what beauties waited for me in the big city?

By the time I got to college, Maureen was just a story I told. The thing about breaking your neck is it humbles you in a hurry. It's hard staying arrogant when you have a halo brace screwed into your skull, when a nurse comes each morning to empty your catheter bag, when your father pulls your lip down so he can brush the bottom teeth. By the time I realized that I might have missed a real catch in Maureen, I didn't want to interfere with my favorite memory.

That Monday morning I decided such hesitation was cowardice. I was going to find her. All I knew was her Christian name and her teenage face, but I had a plan.

It was October and only one cloud stretched across the morning sky, a fish-skeleton floating toward the western horizon. I drove to the supermarket in my new Toyota Land Cruiser and bought a bag of Hershey's Kisses as good-luck charms. Returning to my car I saw a record store in the same strip mall, so I went in and bought *London Calling* on compact disk. Joe Strummer's guitar still sounded good and I thumped the steering wheel with the palms of my hands as I got on Route 202 and headed west. After crossing the Delaware I stopped in New Hope and tracked down Thomas Sweet's. I paid for my ice cream with cash this time and ate it while staring through the windows of the ubiquitous antiques shops. Antiques still bored me, I was relieved to note.

North Wales was as I remembered it, except that the hardware store and the ninety-nine-cent store were gone, replaced by a Sam's Club. I drove out of town to where the farmland began, hoping to see the exact spot where I had first met Maureen on her bicycle. It took me five minutes to realize there was no chance I would find it. And what if I did? What was I expecting to discover there, a bronze marker commemorating the meeting?

I drove back into town and stopped at the barbershop. Inside the barber sat alone on his swivel chair, reading the newspaper. He stood up when I entered and gestured for me to sit. I wished that I needed a cut, the barber could have used the business, but I'd had one a few days before.

"I'm just looking for the high school," I told him. "You know where the high school is?"

"Which high school you want? Kulpsville?"

"Isn't this North Wales?"

"Sure is," said the barber. "But there's no high school here. Nearest one's in Kulpsville. Just hit the 202 north a couple miles. You'll see the clock tower from the road."

When I got to Kulpsville High the day had gotten warm enough for me to leave my coat in the car. The football field lay adjacent to the parking lot, the cheerleaders were practicing, and I thought, hey, cheerleaders. I walked over to watch. The way I walk these days, most people can't tell I ever had a bad accident. My strides are shorter than they used to be, and my back gets stiff when I'm tired, forcing me to shuffle along like an old man, but for the most part I make my way without much trouble.

A few lanky boys were sprawled in the bleachers, drinking Yoo-Hoo, flicking the bottle caps with their thumbs and catching them. They watched me approach.

"How's it going?" I asked, sitting down in the front row.

The boy sitting closest to me wore sunglasses and a beaded necklace and had bleached-blond hair. He wasn't planning on saying anything but I stared at him until he mumbled, "What's up?"

I realized that I was being an asshole, that I didn't belong here, that I had been a cool kid once but that didn't matter at all to the new cool kids. So I waved good-bye to the boys and could feel them watching me, wondering what that had been about. I walked onto the football field. The cheerleaders, phalanxed on the cinder track, stared at me suspiciously. The smell of cut grass, the painted yard markers, the cleat marks in the turf—it had been a long time since I stood on a gridiron. The scoreboard still recorded last week's game: Marauders 17, Visitors 0. The local boys played good defense.

Inside the school building was the old familiar smell: sweating adolescents, ammonia, drying paint, coffee, chalk dust, and chewing gum. The entry hall served as a large tro-phy room, glass cases filled with tarnished bowls and stat-uettes, plaques on the walls commemorating athletes now dead or middle-aged. Carved pumpkins grinned at me from the window ledges and the doorways were trimmed with orange-and-black crepe paper. I walked down carpeted corri-dors and up narrow staircases, the wooden banisters bur-nished by thousands of children's palms. The walls on the second floor were festooned with old photographs: team pic-tures, class pictures, ornately framed portraits of dead teach-ers. There were hooks for hanging book bags, red exit signs, ancient water fountains.

At last I found the library, a cramped room featuring a short row of bookshelves and lead-glass windows that hadn't been washed in years. Students pretending to read squirmed in plastic chairs that lined the walls. The librarian sat at her desk, inserting new magazines into plastic covers. She was young and clean-looking, her black bangs cut straight across her forehead like the hairstyle of Chinese girls you see in old pictures. She smiled up at me.

"Could you tell me where to find the old yearbooks?" I asked her.

"Of course," she said, standing up. "Alumnus?"

"Excuse me?"

"Did you graduate from Kulpsville? I was a '90."

I wanted to tell her that I knew what alumnus meant, that her one-word question had confused me as it might have confused many intelligent men, but I just said, "No, I'm looking for a friend."

She nodded as if people constantly came to her looking for old friends, as if that were her real job and the Dewey decimal system and snot-nosed kids were just a cover. I followed her to the back of the library where she unlocked a door and led me into a dusty inventory room. Cardboard boxes sat on metal shelves. She knelt down beside a stack of yearbooks.

"*The Kulpsville Marauder*, 1959 through 1998. What year did your friend graduate?"

"Around 1987 or 1988, I guess."

She pulled out four yearbooks and handed them to me. "He'll probably be in one of these, then. What's his last name?"

"Her last name. I don't know. That's what I'm looking for."

The librarian laughed. "The two of you aren't very close, I take it."

"We were for a while," I said.

She told me to take as much time as I needed and then left me alone. I wondered if the Mahlus High librarian would be as friendly to Maureen if she came looking for me. I placed the four yearbooks on one of the metal shelves and started paging through the 1987 edition. Whenever possible I work standing up—sitting puts too much pressure on my spine. Even if I wanted to I could no longer drive all the way to California.

There was no way of knowing if Maureen had attended Kulpsville, but it was the best chance I had. I glanced at each senior portrait quickly, all the eager white faces staring up at me, the boys in jackets and ties, the girls in dresses with their hair all done up. None of them were Maureen, so I turned to the 1988 edition and started on the new batch of seniors. Adams, Allison, Appleton, Bardovi, Besser, Bischof—there she was. Maureen Black. She smiled with her mouth closed to hide her chipped teeth. Her freckles were invisible in the black-and-white photograph and she looked more elegant than I had remembered. Below her name was a concise summary of her high school career: *Soccer (captain) 1,2,3,4. Cross-country 1,2,3,4. French Club 3,4. Literary Guild 3,4. Photo Club 4. Casino Club (founder and president) 1,2,3,4. . . . Minx and Lan we're finally gone! Peace to FXO and SB! JJ, you're guilty, fess up . . . MB: 'if a double-decker bus crashes into us . . . ' Thank you Coach Smith for everything . . . Mrs. Wilder, you were right, blue skies ahead! Au revoir, Pennsylvania . . .*

I know I'm a fool but I wanted to see myself in her coded farewell. I wanted to see *LZ: where are you, big man? Rescue me!* But there was no reference to me, as there had been no reference to her in the Mahlus High yearbook. We had come together for an afternoon and that was it.

I replaced the books and returned to the librarian. She smiled up at me again and touched her Chinese bangs. "Did you find your friend?"

"Yeah, thanks. Do you have a phone book handy?"

"Sure." She opened one of her desk drawers and pulled out a thin White Pages. "Who was she, anyway?"

"Maureen Black."

The librarian hesitated and then handed me the phone book, as if she were giving me something very valuable and she wasn't sure that I was trustworthy. "Maureen Black? Class of '88?"

"Yeah, you know her?"

She stared at me for a second before speaking. "That girl died years ago."

I turned to the B pages and started looking for Black. "I don't think so," I said.

"I knew Maureen Black," she said softly. "I played soccer with her. She was murdered by her boyfriend in Las Vegas."

I glanced around and saw that all of the students in the library were watching us. They gripped their pens and listened to our conversation. Above the librarian's desk hung a poster of a muscle-bound cartoon superhero wearing a purple uniform emblazoned with lightning bolts. He held one finger to his lips. *Shhh!!!* read the legend below him. Everyone in the room was hushed, waiting.

"That's not true."

"I'm sorry," said the librarian. "It was big news around here. You can look it up in the microfiche if you'd like. We have *The Montgomery County Sun* for the past—"

I dropped the phone book on her desk and the noise echoed through the room. "You're lying."

The librarian stood up, walked around her desk, touched my elbow. "Let's talk outside for a minute."

"Maureen Black is alive."

She shook her head. "Her boyfriend strangled her and then shot himself. It was in all the papers. Her mom lives over in North Wales. Honestly, it's not the kind of thing I'd make up."

"Take it back."

The librarian's mood was changing. Her natural inclina-
tion to sympathy was giving way to something closer to
fear. She took a step away from me and I knew that my size
was beginning to register on her. The anger was racing
through my body, carried in the blood, coiling in the muscles. I could feel the old power return. I wanted to tear the
school building down, to rest my hands against the support
walls and push, keep pushing until everything collapsed, until all of us were crushed beneath the falling masonry.

"Take it back," I said to the librarian.

She held up her hands as if I were pointing a gun at her.
"Sir? Please, I'm not sure what you want."

"She's alive," I said quietly. "She lives in Las Vegas. She's
the best blackjack dealer in the city."

"Okay."

"Say it."

"Sir—"

"Say it or I'll break your fucking arm."

There were tears in the librarian's eyes. She searched the
room to see if any of the students were going to help her.
One of them was thinking about it, a thick-necked kid in a
denim jacket, but when I looked at him he slid back in his
chair and lowered his eyes.

"She's alive," said the librarian, her voice trembling. "She
lives in Las Vegas."

"And she's never coming back to Pennsylvania. You'll
never see her again."

The librarian started to repeat that, too, but I left her
standing there, surrounded by her books and magazines and
gawking students.

Walking out of the school I kept expecting a security guard to lay hands on me. I would have thrown him through a wall. Nobody approached me. I pushed open the front doors, went back to my car and drove home, the unopened bag of Kisses in the passenger seat.

Maureen was a fighter. She would have kicked him and bit his wrist and clawed at his face. She must have known what was happening. There must have been a moment when she saw her lover's face change, when he ceased to be her lover and all recognition faded from his eyes, when all the complexities burned away and he wanted nothing except to end her. He must have slammed her against the wall, his hands squeezing her throat tighter and tighter, until finally she must have quit, even Maureen must have quit, as the piss streamed down her legs and her lips turned blue and her feet stopped kicking.

I still can't get that picture out of my head. When I come home from work I turn on the TV and watch sports highlights and drink beer and I cannot get that picture out of my head. It makes me hate my own mind, this sick mind, conjuring an image I have never seen and haunting me with it. I *knew* the living girl, her chipped-tooth smile, her jinni's laugh, but I can only imagine her now in agony, stripped of dignity—the gruesome last pages of a story I should have stopped reading in the middle. If I hadn't gone back to North Wales, Maureen would still be alive; she would have survived in my ignorance and prospered.

I didn't tell my father the story of my ride with Maureen in the Eldorado until I was lying in a hospital bed with a broken neck. Dad knew Dr. Byrnes and he would have been furious to hear that I stole the man's car for a day. But after the accident, when dad took a sabbatical from work so that he could be with me, we talked about all sorts of things that never would have come up otherwise. I learned about the girlfriends he had before mom; and what it was like growing up Polish in an Italian neighborhood in Brooklyn; and about the best man at my parents' wedding, who was killed in Vietnam, and whom I was named after.

So I told my father about taking the car from Tommy, and dad shook his head but then he laughed. "I always wanted to drive that car."

I told him the whole story, and when I got to the part about the refrigerator lying in the middle of the road, and how I dodged it at the last second and then warned the guy driving behind me, my father asked, "And then you went back for it?"

"What?"

"You went back and moved the refrigerator out of the way?"

I had been telling the story for five years and nobody had ever asked me that.

"Dad," I said, "it was a huge refrigerator."

He looked at me in the hospital bed, my shrunken body, the halo brace screwed into my skull, and then he looked out the window. "You could have moved it."

I could have. I wonder how many other drivers swerved around it without stopping, congratulating themselves on their fine reflexes. I wonder if that evening a young man sped over the dark country road, toward a girlfriend he would never kiss, toward a collision he would never see coming.

DE COMPOSITION

Winter, and the bombs are falling. Safe here, safe for now, twelve feet below the dead grass, twelve feet of concrete, lead and topsoil between the explosions and me. My food and water supplies were to last for eighteen months, according to earlier estimates, but those calculations are no longer valid. I am constantly thirsty.

When news of the initial hostilities came over my radio, the announcer's voice lowered by the occasion's gravity (I imagined him alone in the studio, a heroic figure bravely manning the microphone), I gathered the final requisites from my house and proceeded to the backyard toolshed, where my shelter's hatch is concealed from the eyes of strangers. All the neighbors knew that my hideaway existed; covert excavation proved impossible. They mocked my midnight burrowings, of course, but good-naturedly, coming out onto their porches to watch my labors. Three years of spare time produced this bunker, and all the work my own: the wiring, the ventilation, the closed-cycle plumbing unit. Great entertainment for the neighbors. I was the local lunatic, but harmless, and they took some pride in my madness. Save room for me, they would shout, grinning down from the hatchway as I toiled below, pouring concrete or laying pipe. In the final months, as overseas disturbances flared into battles, as the rhetoric escalated from warnings to ultimatums to declarations, as the possibility of peaceful resolution began to fade, the neighbors pretended they were not concerned, smiled at my hysteria, attempted to convince me that my fears were imagined. Don't forget the can opener, they would shout, and laugh. I did not forget the can opener. I sit here, twelve feet below their ashes, and pray they died painlessly.

· · ·

Every morning I wake to limited prospects. My bunker is gray concrete. The walls are separated by five strides. Early in the war I followed a rigorous exercise schedule, a brutal series of push-ups, sit-ups, and deep knee bends designed to maintain fighting form in case I had to defend my shelter from intruders and, equally important, to combat the adverse physical effects of voluntary captivity. But several months ago I decided that the increased caloric demands of such rigorous exertion, and the consequent depletion of my larder, posed a more immediate threat than sloth. And I no longer fear the attentions of survivors.

Time has become a game for me. The objective is night and the comfort of sleep; the obstacles are the hours. Each day is divided into tightly scheduled periods—any deviation from routine results in mandatory punishment: a spoonful less protein supplement, for example, or, if the violation was particularly egregious, confiscation of my weekly chocolate bar.

The early morning is devoted to an extensive revie1w of my facility's equipment. The air filters, water tank, generator, and closed-cycle plumbing must be constantly inspected, cleaned, and, when the situation warrants, repaired. Out of necessity I have become an expert repairman, master of all my machines.

Electricity is a luxury. A single fluorescent bulb lights my space, but only when required. I eat in darkness, I meditate in darkness, I perform my infrequent bowel movements in darkness. When I work at the computer, as now, the monitor provides sufficient illumination for typing. The machine drains a great deal of energy. Only one hour of operation per day is permitted, and that is the favorite hour. All other hours are servants, scrubbing and scouring in preparation for the coming time, the sixty minutes of blue light. A portion of the good hour is reserved for writing, transcribing the lines that have already been scratched out on paper with a pencil, or, more frequently now, composed in my mind. Due to a procurement error, only one pencil was interred with me; the yellow wood has been whittled down to a matchstick. But as is so often the case, deprivation inspires greater efficiency. I recite the words I plan to type, measuring the syntax, securing whole passages in memory's vault.

When the time comes I write as quickly as possible, saving the day's pages with a push of the button. One unforeseen advantage of the war is that my computer, Model

1468, top of the line when I bought it, will remain top of the line. No new technology will supplant it (I resist the traditional *her* reserved for favored machines; the sleek curves of a roadster or sailboat might suggest femininity, but nothing about the 1468 does). My computer will never be obsolete, will never be humbled by an endless succession of snickering progeny, memories doubling every generation.

Once the scheduled writing has been completed (twenty minutes on a typical day), the best part of the best hour begins, and I read. Early in the planning stages of my bunker, 0I realized that there would not be enough room for my books. My space is severely cramped; every cubic foot is precious. The solution presented itself as technology advanced: an entire library now fits on a single optical disc. Tap a few keys and I am privy to the ruminations of Hamlet, the manipulations of Odysseus, the risen Beatrice. An entire civilization is preserved below ground, the best thoughts of the best minds reified by laser.

Why read these decomposed authors? Because only the dead can save us. Only they can teach us how to rebuild our broken cities. I believe that all our fallen fathers will rise again and hold our dwindling bodies in mighty hands.

· · ·

A significant problem of permanent reclusion is the lack of sexual outlets. I considered purchasing a pornographic disc for my computer, but decided such activity would distract me from my mission. Thousands of hours of solitude have led me to curse my priggish stance, have left me feverishly conjuring images of nude bodies. Strangely, I find that I am unable to remember faces; my imagined nymphs are crudely drawn. There are few things more likely to demolish a man's morale than failed masturbation.

In desperation I have turned to a disc that came with my 1468, an introduction to human biology that includes some fairly stimulating studies of naked females. Many of these ladies, unfortunately, are attractive on the left side but transparent on the right, revealing the detailed workings of their inner organs, a view certain to repel all but the most perverse suitors.

Then yesterday (O lucky day!) I stumbled upon an appendix to an anatomy primer, a fitness regimen specifying appropriate nutrition and exercises for the middle-aged, detailed diagrams accompanied by wondrous prose, including my current inamorata:

> *This gentle rhythmic action helps to lift and firm flabby buttocks. The effective movement tones and tightens muscles in the buttocks and hips as well as strengthening the stomach muscles by resistance tension.*
> *INSTRUCTIONS—BEGINNER*
> * *Lie on back with buttocks on moving pads.*
> * *Extend legs with knees slightly bent.*
> * *Press flexed feet against side pads.*
> * *Perform a pelvic tilt.*
> * *Keep stomach and buttocks tight.*

In all my reading I have come across no phrase as arousing as that final demand for tightened buttocks. The instructions form a bildungsroman of sorts, progressing from the flabby novice of the opening to the tight, pelvic-tilting performer of the close.

I was not always this pathetic.

. . .

The most malicious aspect of extended confinement is the aural hallucinations, the ghost cries of a dead civilization. Some mornings I could swear I hear the sounds of honking cars, and I have been awakened several times by an insistent rapping on the hatch door, followed by a perfect imitation of children's laughter. My mind, buried below the dead, creates a mirage of noise, human voices replacing palm trees and watering holes. Like an amputated foot that continues to itch, my obliterated town still echoes above me.

. . .

I am well aware of the warren of underground chambers secretly constructed by my government for the protection and wartime comfort of our leaders. No doubt the major corporations followed suit, carving boardrooms in the bedrock. Even now gray-suited analysts meet in well-appointed caverns to discuss the ramifications of an incinerated consumer base.

Others will survive this calamity, but only those deemed vital by their respective masters: the necessary bureaucrats, soldiers, scientists, engineers. Who will tell the story of our civilization's end? I should01er that task, though I am a reticent man by nature.

My approach must be microhistorical, for I have no access to the primary documents that papered the path to this fiery place. All I know is my own life, and that is all I can relate. Future scholars must extrapolate an entire society from a single man. I leave this journal as an heirloom for the unborn, that they might learn what went wrong this time, that I might serve and survive as a voice crying out from the ruins. In black ink my name may still shine bright.

The relevance of the following material will have to be sorted out later. Truth might be stranger than fiction, but it needs a better editor. The greater part of anyone's lifetime is not worth remembering.

· · ·

The first horror. Four years old, on my knees by the side of the bed, saying my evening prayers. When I finished I opened my eyes and saw, through the window's glass, a man with a terribly burned face staring back at me. I ran to my parents' room. For a minute I could not work my mouth, but finally I told them what I had seen. My father joked with me, telling me how trees look human in the dark. He switched on the outdoor lights and stepped outside. I wanted him to stay, was certain the burned man would hack him to bits, but my father only laughed. When he came back inside he was grim-faced, slid the dead bolt into place, left the outdoor lights burning. My mother asked him what was wrong and he muttered that there were footsteps in the snow. She called the police while he went upstairs for his shotgun.

Nothing happened. They never found the burned man. No lunatics were missing from asylums, no convicts escaped from death row, nobody was murdered in our town. But that terrible face, two eyes trapped within ruined skin, cannot be forgotten. I wonder how many like him now wander our country's roads, tattered men crying out for water.

. . .

Do you recognize her, that woman bald and bawling? She is your mother. For nearly ten months you dwelled within her, and only left because the doctors smoked you out. This becomes family legend, the boy who did not want to be born.

She was a beautiful woman, my mother, and strong, and I don't know why I cannot remember her as beautiful and strong. Every time I picture her face I picture her dying face, the tendons in her neck bulging through the skin, her teeth dug into her upper lip. All your life you know a person, and love her, and then in the space of a year sickness boils her down to her bones. Perhaps I should be grateful that she was not alone in the end. So many die without our caring, decline to silence in rooms beyond hearing. We honor the dead and abhor the dying.

Pain gradually erased my mother's fine complexities, left her curled in a hospital bed, trying to twist away from the clawing inside her. And what can you do? Your mother is slowly murdered and you sit, powerless, and watch. It ends with horror, it ends with the brain starved for oxygen, with the lips gone blue and the feet swelled with fluid. It ends when a mother's eyes become the eyes of fish. Billions of times this ritual repeated, billions of sons watched their mothers die, kissed their cold foreheads, and wept.

If grief was pure, things would be easier, but there is a selfishness in mourning, and a degree of disgust for those still living and cheerful. The diversions of friends seem moronic and irritating, their love lives ridiculous, their complaints petty. Nothing can compete with grief and the griever knows it, and no matter how far into the depths he might fall, he still looks down at the ignorant hordes who cannot see death all around them.

And how did this loss shape my character? Just tap the proper keys and the answer will emerge, correct? Enough of this. No more writing tonight. The issue of my mother is better off filed away.

. . .

There is nothing beautiful left in the world, nothing above but skeletons: skeletons strolling down the sidewalk, skeletons washing their cars, skeletons dancing in the late-night dance halls, skeletons drinking their whiskey straight, skeletons bluffing with a single suicide king, skeletons scratching on the eight-ball, skeletons humping in the courtyard, skeletons eating with fork and knife, skeletons singing lullabies to their skeletal babes.

And those who find me, what will they think? They will dig up my bones in three thousand years and wonder, what strange beast was this?

. . .

We begin with Prometheus. The Titan chained to a great rock, punishment for bringing fire to the humans. Every day a vulture swoops down and devours his liver. The pain, we are meant to understand, is unbearable. The moral is spelled clearly for the dullards among us: stay within thy boundaries.

But can sensation maintain its clarity for eternity? Eventually Prometheus stops screaming. He retreats inward from the pain, after years, or decades, or centuries. The suffering is suppressed, locked in a trunk in the attic of consciousness. But Prometheus is still chained to a rock. And so he begins to imagine, to dream of freedom. Let it be so. He creates fictional cities and roams through them, drinks in fictional taverns, consorts with fictional lovers. And in one of these strange cities, walking at dusk down a desolate avenue along the abandoned docks, the transformation occurs: Prometheus is no longer aware of his fiction—the fiction has swallowed him whole. Let it be so. The street signs are stamped in the machinery of his mind, but he is not conscious of their creation. And the beings created now populate an entire world, a universe, convinced of their own reality—even their creator is convinced of their reality. We're all waking in the Titan's dream.

Substitute the word *God* for *Prometheus* and *loneliness* for the *vulture*. Genesis begins with torture, whether a vulture's beak or infinite loneliness, the face of the One moving over dark waters. To those who ask, "Where is God now?" I respond, "He has forgotten that He exists."

. . .

Catastrophe. My computer's security scan has detected a virus. I have no 1connection to the outside world—there *is* no outside world—so I must presume that the rogue code was transmitted by my optical discs, or else was programmed into my 1468 at birth. The closed-cycle plumbing unit. Great entertainment for the neighbors. I was the local lunatic, scanning function recognized the virus and even has a name for it: "Air Dred." What possesses people to sabotage the unseen work of strangers? The hacker who created Air Dred must have stalked the museums of the world, slashing the canvases caloric demands of such rigorous exertion, and the consequent depletion of my larder, posed a caloric demands of such rigorous exertion, and the consequent depletion of my larder, posed a of Old Masters. Dark days for me: My life preserver has sprung a leak.

· · ·

Still trying to determine the extent of the damage. The 1468's security system identifies intruders and attempts to neutralize them but refuses to provide any useful information concerning the saboteur's methods. Air Dred is a "memory-site infection": that is the extent of my knowledge. My computer has a tumor, the tumor is malig01nant, should all countermeasures fail the tumor will metastasize, my computer will die. This reeks of melodrama, granted, but I am lost without 1468. The computer is my companion, my library, the record of my days. Without it I am faced with uninterrupted solitude. And what could I contemplate to lift and firm flabby buttocks in those silent hours but personal extinction? It will be as if I never was. Drowned, all my plans to serve as a bottled message, to provide the blueprints of our Atlantis to future divers.

Still, no need for panic yet. I have confidence in my 1468's autosurgery. Humanity's greatest talent is you know a person, and love them, and then in the space of a year sickness boils them down to their bones. Perhaps I should be grateful that she was not alone in the end. So many die without our caring, decline to silence in rooms beyond hearing. We surviving. We will rule this planet until something better comes along.

. . .

I don't know what I1010was thinking, refusing to die with my tribe. Sheer conceit that it could matter at all, this dismal little man stabbing at keys in near darkness, twelve feet below01 the ground. The sentence I wish could end this journal—Spring, and the grass is rising—will never truthfully be written. I could live one hundred years and never survive this winter.

Words fail me, it goes without saying. Yes, it does. Gone and unsaid.

. . .

Mostly I miss the nighttime, walking through grass fields lit by stars alive and dying and dead. And lying down in the woods beyond the town limits, lulled by the deceitful I perform my infrequent bowel movements in darkness. When I work I perform my infrequent bowel movements in darkness. When I work I perform my infrequent bowel movements in darkness. When I work I perform my infrequent bowel movements in darkness. When I work I perform my infrequent bowel movements in darkness. When I work harmony surrounding me. Every tree battle101d toward the sun, leaving its neighbor to wither in the shade; the hooting owl is waiting with hooked claws for a shrew to break cover; the cricket heard fiddling is the lone survivor of a three-thousand brood, her brothers and sisters murdered by frost and frogs.

T001010his world was at war long before us.

· · ·

I am losing everything. Air Dred advances on every front,1a0digital blitzkrieg swarming past all defenses. 1468 no longer retrieves previously saved documents. There is no way of knowing whether the computer's memory preserves anything I type. No way of knowing whether my memories are remembered by 01101468. I came down here to tell my stories but my stories are swallowed whole by a sick machine.

And my library, all my beautiful books, deathless, I thought, deathless, but I've lost them, Homer and Dante and Shakespea01001re01and00Cervantes and Goethe and what strange beast was this? Shelley and Baudelaire and Tolstoy, gone, all of them, buried below a snow of zeros and ones. Leaving me alone at last, all my truest friends, the heroes and villains of a thousand novels, plays and poems, all the creations of all the wonderful minds slaughtered by a mindless virus, the imagined city emptied by plague.

Will anyone read this? Who could I be writing for, what possible au11010010dience still there were footsteps in the snow. She called there were footsteps in the snow. She called there were footsteps in the snow. She called there were footsteps in the snow. She called there were footsteps in the snow. She called there were footsteps in the snow. She called there were footsteps in the snow. She called there were footsteps in the snow. She called there were footsteps in the snow. She called there were footsteps in the snow. She called there were footsteps in the snow. She called there were footsteps in the snow. She called there were footsteps in the snow. She called exists?

I need to escape. This gray box I am trapped in shrinks

every day, the blocks of concrete edging closer, squeezing out the air. Need to flee, need to run as fast as I can for as long as I want.

I am nothing but an eschatologist of the underground, not even bright enough to realize that the conclusion has already been written and I am101000marching in lockstep from left to right, trapped in a text that offers no exit but the end.

· · ·

Again today the knocking on my hatch door, insistent this time, lasting fifteen minutes. My mind is beginning to defo1011011rm.010Or has something survived? And if so, do I dare to open the hatch? Anything that dwells in the fiction has swallowed him whole. The street signs are stamped in the machinery of his mind, but he is not conscious of the fiction has swallowed him whole. The street signs are stamped in the machinery of his mind, but he is not conscious of the wasteland above must be desperate, scavenging for f110ood and drinkable water. A horde of interlopers could easily overpower m01e, seize me by the neck and drag me from safety. Maybe the survivo110110101rs01have110reverted to cannibalism; they will tie me to a tree and carve open my belly with linoleum knives looted from the hardware store, fry my intestines on an open fire while 0I still live.

Hours have passed since the knocking stopped. I very nearly unlatched the hatch a few minutes ago, but decided against it. For one thing, I dete0110101100101 00100110110rmined from the beginning to remain underground at least six months, as a precaution against radioactive fallout. Beyond that is the fear of what I will see, the ruins of my hometown, all my landmarks rubbl0100e.

But there is a deeper dread, scurrying about on tiny clawed feet below the floorboards of my mind, that 0I will emerge from this bunker and find everything untouched, the same houses clad in the same fiberglass siding, th011e same lawns still littered with inflatable pools and children's toys, the same neighbors gathered for their Sunday barbecue, drinking cans of beer and shooing away the horseflies.

· · ·

This morning I rediscovered hope—I believe I have fou0110nd a01way to de1101feat Air Dred. I01f0011

my101pl0110101010an11010110100101101011011011s10
1101001110101011u001011101001101001110010c10110
0011100100101101011010111000101101010101001100110
11000100110011001c0101101001011001010101010101100
1100110010011101001111000101101011010010100111001
1011010011001010010100101010101001110100100111ee
0101011001010110110101001111010111011001110111001
101101011011101010111011010100110111001011010110
101110110110011011011001111001011010110101010110
1011101010010101010011110110110101101010l0101010110
1001011100110010110101100011101001011001011101001
1010011101001010110001110010010110101010111001001
11010101001101011011000001100110101010010010110010
1010010101100110011001001110100111100010110101101
00100011100110110001101010010100011110011101001001
11100101011l000011011010100111101011101100111101110
01101011011011101010111011100011011100111010111011
0111011011001101101100111100101101011010101101101
01110101001010101001101011010100011010100111001010
0101100101101010001101010011101010010110010110101

00011010100111010100101100101101010001101010011 10
10100101100101101010001101010011101010010110010 11
01010001101010011101010010110010110101000110101 00
11101010010110010110101000110101001110101001011 00
10110101000110101001110101001011011011011010110 10
11010101100011110101100101101011000111010010110 01
01110100110100111010010101100I0111001001011000101
11000011101010100110011011000001100110010100100 10
11010101010001011001100110010011101001111000101 10
10110100100011100110110001101010010100011110011 10
10010011100101011000011011010100111101011101100 11
10101100110110101101111010101110111000111110011 101
01010101011101101100110110110011011001011010110 10
10110110101110101001010101001111011011010110101 10
10101100011011010110010110101100011101001011001 01
11010011010011101001010110001110010010110001011 10
00011101010100110011011000001100111011000110101 00
10100011110011101001001110010101100001100100111 00
10101100001100100111001010110000110010011100101 01
10000110010011100101011000011001001110010101100 00
11001001110010101100001100100111001010110000110 01
00111001010110000110010011100101011000011001001 11
00101011000011001001110010101100001100100111001 01
01100001100100111001010110000110010011100101011 00
00110010011100101011000011001001110010101100001 10
01001110010101100001100100111001010110000110010 01
00110010011100101011000011001001110010101100001 10
01001110010101100001100100111001010110000110010 01
11001010110000110010011100101011000011001001110 00

GARDEN OF NO

He was a poet. Burn scars covered his forearms. Whenever the hot grease leapt from the grill to bite him, he'd step back, wipe his arm across his dirty white apron, and stare at the sizzling burgers like a man betrayed. The first time I saw this happen I ran to the ice machine for an ice cube, came back and pressed it against the angry red splotch on his skin. He watched me, smiling. He had the darkest eyes of any white man I've ever known, and the biggest hands.

That was my first day waiting tables at Wiley's. After the lunch rush was over he took his break and came out to the counter for a cup of coffee. I filled his cup and he smiled at me. Sam wasn't an especially handsome man, but when he smiled you wanted to stay with him, to lean back and bathe for a while. After a long day on your feet, Sam was like a tub of warm water.

"So I hear you're an actress."

Yes, I was a waitress, and yes, I wanted to be an actress. I would meet people at parties and tell them I was a waitress, and they would always ask, "But you want to be an actress?" As if they were so original, these publicists and software designers and production supervisors.

There was no point burdening Sam with these gripes, so I said, "I'm trying."

"You look a little like Cassie Whitelaw. People ever tell you that?"

I groaned. "All the time. I wish I had her plastic surgeon."

Cassie Whitelaw, star of the hospital drama *St. James Infirmary*, was my personal nemesis, the beautiful version of me. When I first saw her, in a television ad for dandruff shampoo, it was funny. We were watching the Oscars and all my friends cackled and threw popcorn at me. Now, with her magazine covers and visits with Jay Leno and movie star boyfriend, she's not funny anymore. I saw her one time on the Third Street Promenade and followed her past the movie theaters and sports bars and sidewalk saxophonists, watching her skinny ankles and lizard-skin pumps, watching the promenaders recognize her and nudge each other, watching her bask in the watching.

Sam said, "Nah, you're prettier than her."

• • •

The first morning at Sam's I woke to clacking, loud and unsteady, like shots fired from a capgun. I staggered to the bathroom, opened the door, and flinched as the sunlight attacked me. Below the bright window sat Sam, on the closed toilet seat, an old manual typewriter on his lap. The typewriter looked like a toy in his giant hands. He wore plaid boxers and an L.A. Raiders T-shirt and a ridiculous pair of horn-rim glasses.

"Sorry," he said. "Did I wake you?"

"What are you doing?" I was shielding my eyes with my hand, trying not to imagine what I looked like right then, what kind of monster risen from the deep I most resembled.

"If I don't get my writing done in the morning, I don't get it done. It's a poem."

"A poem? You write poems?"

"Yes," he said, and there was both pride and resignation in the way he said it. "Yes, I do."

"Oh" is what I said. Mostly I wanted to escape the sunlight. There was something wonderful and admirable about a man who wrote poetry in the morning, but something embarrassing as well, and I wanted to go back to bed, to my own bed.

. . .

My mother did not approve of the Sam situation.

"What does he do?"

"He's a poet."

Silence on the line. "But what does he really do?"

"I'm telling you, he's a poet."

"All right. And what does he do for money?"

I sighed. "He's a short-order cook."

"Thank you," she said. "And how old is he?"

"Thirty-five."

"Oh, thirty-five. Well, that's nice. So this is what he wants to be, a short-order cook? He's happy with that?"

"I don't know about happy. It's a job. It pays the rent."

"June—"

"He can bring home the bacon," I said, and then I laughed and laughed. It was an old joke of Sam's. I laughed and laughed, not because it was so funny, but because the longer I laughed, the longer I could put off listening to my mother.

"Wonderful," she said, when I finally stopped. "That's wonderful."

. . .

In the middle of May everything changed. My agent called after months of silence and I asked him if he had the wrong phone number. He laughed and said, "Nah, champ, I've been waiting for the perfect part. No use dragging you to a lot of calls if the part's not you. This one's got your name all over it."

I pictured *June* scrawled one hundred times on a blackboard. *June will never get this part. June will never get this part.* After seven years of close calls and bad luck, I had learned to treat hope as a dangerous emotion, the mother of all suffering. But I called Showfax and had them fax the sides to a mailbox store on my block. Two of my friends came over and read with me until my timing was perfect. My agent was right: The part had been written for me. Linda McCoy, the third biggest role in *Joe's Eats*, was a wisecracking waitress at a greasy spoon. Somebody in power was having a little joke, and I was happy to play along.

On a Tuesday morning I read for the casting director's assistant. She was about my age and prettier, and she fed me lines in a robotic monotone that seemed calculated to throw me off my stride. But I was strong. I was Linda McCoy. By the end of the scene the casting director's assistant was giggling despite herself.

They gave me a callback and a week later I read for the casting director, and a week after that for the producers.

Bucky Lefschaum, the man who created *Mr. Midnight* and *The Campus Green*, a man I'd seen cavorting with the stars at the Golden Globe Awards, stood up in the middle of my read. His curly hair was fading from his forehead but he was fit and tanned. He looked like the tennis pro that all the country club wives were fucking.

"Stop," he said. He took off his sunglasses and hooked the stem in the collar of his polo shirt. "Just stop right there. Why go on? You *are* Linda McCoy. You're my girl."

He shook my hand and left, just like that. I turned to the casting director.

"I got the part?"

"Not yet," he said. "You still have to read for the network."

"Mazel tov," said my agent when I told him the news. "If Lefschaum liked you, you're golden. Just look as good as possible for the network. That's all they care about. What do they know about acting?"

I read for the network in a conference room at their studio in Century City. Framed posters of sitcom stars hung from the walls, flashing bleached teeth and airbrushed cleavage. The producers, including Bucky Lefschaum, sat on one side of the table. The network executives sat on the other side. It was casual Friday and it was beach weather, the stupid Los Angeles sun beaming its indiscriminate love on everyone, and the executives wore short sleeves. They were much younger than I had imagined. I only recognized one name, Elliot Cohen, the senior vice president of something. He slouched in the corner wearing faded corduroys and a linen shirt, with a surfer's lean body and freefalling hair. I recognized his name because he was a well-known Hollywood swordsman, notorious for sleeping with two of the three female *Friends*, though at that moment I couldn't remember which two. He was a man of stature in the community. He looked like he would smell good.

I stood at the head of the table in my waitress uniform, cracking my gum and wondering if I could run to the bathroom. I decided it would be a bad idea and tried to ignore the growing pressure in my bladder.

Bucky Lefschaum winked and gave me the thumbs-up. The casting director began feeding me lines. By now I knew the scenes so well I could act them in my sleep, and sometimes did. I did not hold back. The first good sign was my first punch line. Everyone in the room started cracking up. It wasn't even a great line.

The second good sign was the executives' notepads. The network people had their yellow legal pads in front of them, their pens in hand ready to scribble comments. About ten seconds after I started, all their pens were lying on the table, the yellow pages unmarked.

I finished and everyone clapped.

"Well?" asked Bucky Lefschaum. "Did I tell you?"

"That was wonderful, June."

"She'll play off Delilah Cotton perfectly."

"Okay?" asked Bucky. "We have our Linda?"

My eyes were open but I was floating in the ether. All the fear and disappointment and resentment, the years of No, all the alumni magazines featuring all the supreme achievers from my class, all of it flown away from me, leaving me so light that I could not feel my body, could not feel the floor beneath my feet.

"I have a problem."

And just like that I was back in my body, the space walk of a second before a half-remembered psychedelic trip. It was Elliot Cohen with the problem. He leaned back in his chair and rubbed his palm over his stubbled jaw.

"She looks just like Cassie Whitelaw."

"Who?" asked Bucky.

"Jeez," said a lady executive. "She does. I didn't even notice that."

"I'm not getting it," said Bucky. "Who gives a crap about Cassie Whatever?"

"I do," said Cohen. "I'm paid to give a crap. She looks just like Cassie Whitelaw from *St. James Infirmary*."

"So what?"

"It's too confusing for our viewership. People think they're watching a different show."

"What? Your what? Your *viewership*? What is that, Yiddish? Your fucking *viewership*?!"

Bucky Lefschaum, God bless his heart, hollered and cursed for all he was worth. I walked out of the room and kept walking until I found the women's room.

• • •

"It's terrible business," said my agent. "I told them I'm not going to send them actors anymore if this is how they're treated. But, you know, it's a network. They know we can't hold out on them. Anyway, keep your head up, champ. Your ship will come in."

Sam gave me an hour-long massage, kneading the tired muscles in my calves, rubbing the sore spot between my shoulders, kissing the back of my neck.

"Do you know how beautiful you are?" he asked when he was finished, his knees on either side of my belly. "Do you have any idea?"

"Sam?"

"Uh huh?"

"What if someday you wrote the perfect poem—"

"What's the perfect poem?"

"No, just say you wrote the perfect poem. Or, let's say it's a great poem. You know it's a great poem. You're absolutely sure."

"That's the thing, though, with poetry. You're never sure."

"But say this time you are. Okay? Hypothetically, you've written a poem, it's really good, people will be reading it in a thousand years. And you send it off and you wait and you wait and finally one day you open the mailbox and you've got a hundred letters, and each one's a form letter, and each one's saying no."

"Right."

"Well? What would you do?"

"I'd write another poem. Maybe I'd write a poem about getting a hundred rejection letters in one day."

"You're stronger than me, I guess."

"No, I'm not. Here," he said, leaning across the bed and picking up a typed note from the nightstand. "I got one today. You want to hear it?"

I did not want to hear it but Sam had already begun.

"Thank you for sending us your manuscript. The return of your work does not necessarily imply criticism of its merit, but may simply mean that it does not meet our present editorial needs. We regret that circumstances do not allow individual comment. The Editors."

He laughed. "When I die I'm going to find the pearly gates all locked up with a sign saying, We regret that circumstances do not allow individual comment.' "

I reached up and pulled his curly head closer so I could kiss the newborn bald spot.

"You could always come down and keep me company," I told him.

. . .

My agent called a week later. "I just got off the phone with Lefschaum," he told me. *"St. James Infirmary* was canceled."

"Yeah?"

"That means Cassie Whitelaw's off the air. That means they want you."

"Yeah?"

So I finally got my sitcom, playing Linda McCoy at a greasy spoon called Joe's Eats. My boss's name is Mr. Lee, played by a man who really is named Mr. Lee, a famous comedian from China. I hadn't known there were famous comedians from China. When I said that to Sam he laughed at me. "Jesus Christ, June, there's a billion people in China. You don't think any of them are funny?"

I was so used to rejection that when the break finally came—the break I'd been dreaming about for years, asleep and awake—it seemed unreal. In April I was taking orders for turkey melts and fries, by September I was a regular on network television, slinging hash browns and one-liners in 6.5 million homes nationwide.

The night I signed my contracts Sam took me to Dan Tana's to celebrate. He wore a jacket and tie for the first time since I'd met him, and he combed his hair into a careful side-part. Usually when we went out Sam would drop me off at the door and then drive around for ten minutes looking for a space; on this night he turned his car over to the valet and escorted me to the maître d's station.

Once we were seated at our booth Sam ordered a bottle of good champagne, a bottle he couldn't afford, and right then I knew what was going to happen. I saw how nervous he was, playing with his fork, scratching his neck behind the tight collar, gulping down his ice water, and I knew.

After the waiter poured the champagne Sam lifted his glass and said, "To Linda McCoy. May she live a long, happy life."

"To Linda McCoy."

We drank, and when I lowered my glass Sam was still staring at me. I wanted to stop him, I wanted to hold his curly head to my chest and whisper how awful I was, how foul-tempered and jealous, how vain and insecure, a woman who could not be reasonably expected to make anyone happy.

Instead I said nothing, only watched him root around in his jacket pocket. It was like seeing a suicide leap from a tall building—there was so much time to watch him fall, to wonder why he jumped.

Please, Sam, I wanted to say, please don't, please look somewhere else. Because the word was coming and the word was so loud the whole restaurant must already hear it, the word was so loud it drowned out the jazz pouring from the speakers, drowned out all the drunken laughter, all the cell phone conversations, and the diners were elbowing each other and turning this way, Oh, look, look, that poor schmuck, he hasn't got a chance, doesn't he hear it?

The word was No and I was the word made flesh. I was rejection in a Mexican peasant shirt, rubbing the rim of the champagne flute to hear the glass hum. Sam pulled the ring from his pocket and started to slide forward off his banquette. I put my hand on his shoulder and stopped him.

"Sam," I said, and anything more seemed redundant, so I kissed his shaven jaw, stood up, and walked quickly to the door. I thought someone would grab me and force me back to the table, some officer of the law. This could not go unpunished. This was unkindness so deep I wanted to slither free of my skin, drop the husk of me on the floor of the restaurant, and run, my wet skinless feet leaving bloody prints on the sidewalk.

Nobody stopped me and nobody pulled out the flaying knives and I walked for two miles down Santa Monica Boulevard, wishing it would rain so I could at least be the drama queen, sobbing as the mascara ran down my cheeks. The truth was, though, that the farther I walked the better I felt. By the time I got to Fairfax I was singing to myself, old radio tunes and songs I made up on the spot.

Outside of Canter's Deli an old hunched-over bum held

out a Styrofoam cup and jingled his change. "Help me get some dinner, miss?"

"No," I said, forcefully.

I pushed opened the door and walked inside, past the buttery pastries stacked neatly behind glass, and the bum called after me, "Maybe on the way out?"

At my table I ordered matzoh ball soup and cheese blintzes and when the food came I devoured it, wiping my mouth with the back of my hand, spearing pickles from their briny bowl. Around me the young Hollywood hopefuls jabbered away. That was the season for leopard skin and all the girls wore it: leopard-skin coats, leopard-skin pants, leopard-skin thigh-high boots, even one young flirt in a leopard-skin pillbox hat.

The ceiling at Canter's is meant to look like stained glass. It's a strange effect. What's a Jewish delicatessen doing with a fake stained-glass ceiling? But I liked it, I liked the painted branches, the painted blue sky, the soft light that spills down.

The kids around me were loud and obnoxious, howling for the waitress, stomping their boot heels, yelling out insults, jumping from table to table, exchanging phone numbers, bragging about their plans for the weekend. I liked them. They all wanted something and most of them wouldn't get it. I didn't know a single kid in the restaurant but I knew what they were: actors and musicians and writers and comedians and directors. Most of them weren't claiming those professions on their tax returns and most of them never would, but that's what they were. For a few minutes that night I liked all of them. I wanted to protect them. They seemed so young and brave, recklessly assured, so cocky and virile and American. They were all going to be stars and they were practicing their roles, confident that people were watching them, that people cared. They were optimists, and if they weren't optimists they were pretending, and they believed that somewhere a man in a suit was waiting to see their faces or hear their songs or read their scripts, and the man in the suit would nod and say, Yes. Except there aren't enough Yeses to go around.

In the middle of my reverie the girl in the leopard-skin pillbox hat slid into my booth opposite me. She leaned over the bowl of pickles and whispered, "We just want you to know that we think you're the greatest."

I stared at her. Her skin was very pale, almost translucent. I could see the fine network of blue veins traced across her temples. She wore a necklace of paste emeralds.

"Tell me if I'm bugging you," she said quickly. "I'm not a psycho, honest. But we were all watching you and I just had to come over. Is it okay?"

"Sure. Do you want a pickle?"

"I just had four. Why are you eating alone?"

"Well," I said, "my boyfriend just proposed and I ran away. And I was hungry so I came in here."

"Yeah," she said, nodding, as if she'd expected that answer, as if most people at Canter's had just fled marriage proposals. "I think it's a shame, it's *criminal*, that they canceled *St. James Infirmary*. That was the best show ever."

"Oh. *Oh*. Well, thanks. We had fun with it."

"And I just wanted to tell you, and this is from all of

us"—she pointed to her table on the other side of the room and her friends waved at me—"we all think you're really great and you shouldn't be sad because you're going to be fine. We're all big fans. Would it be okay, I know this is really cheesy, I'm sorry, but—"

She held up a ballpoint pen and looked at me nervously.

"It's fine," I said, taking the pen. "What's your name?"

"Mira. M-I-R-A."

I pulled a napkin out of the dispenser and began writing.

"You're an actress, Mira?"

"Yes! I mean, I'm trying. I just got an agent, actually."

"Congratulations." I handed her the napkin and she read it aloud.

"Mira: When you win your Oscar and you're giving your speech, I want you to thank me, and I want you to tell everyone that I said it would happen. Yours, Cassie Whitelaw."

She looked up at me, her brown eyes open wide, her pale skin flushing at the cheeks.

"That's so incredible. Thank you! Do you really think I have a chance?"

"Yes," I told her. "Yes."

NEVERSINK

"I brought his ashes home with me. He wants them tossed in the Neversink. It's illegal, but that's what he wants."

"The Neversink?"

"It's a reservoir," you said. "Up in the Catskills, where he was born."

That was by way of an introduction; that was the night we first met. Michael, already drunk on Scotch, had clamped his palms on the back of our necks and pressed our foreheads together.

"The two of you ought to be friends," he said. He was the birthday boy, so we sat next to each other in the restaurant's backroom and played *what do you do, who do you know*. Except you cheated. You told me that you had just flown back from your father's funeral in L.A.

"How did he die?" I asked. I knew that wasn't a very decorous question but I couldn't help it. That's what I always want to know, how the dead got dead.

You tilted a red candle so that the wax poured onto my palm. "Does that hurt?"

"No," I lied.

"You have a high tolerance for pain, Frank. I like that."

"Frankie," I said. I do have a high tolerance for pain. That's not the same as liking pain.

"He died of lung cancer, Frankie. He smoked four packs a day."

I had never heard of anyone smoking four packs a day. "I'm sorry," I said. It seemed like the wrong time to say "I'm sorry," but I knew those words were required at some point in any conversation about a dead relative, and I figured I ought to fit them in while I had the chance.

"It was like," you said, and then paused. "It was like he was trying to burn himself down."

I played with the wax in my hand and said nothing. Nobody in my family was dead and I had a hard time imagining them dead.

There were twenty of us crowded into the narrow backroom. Crooked red candles burned on the long, yellowclothed table; fake zebra skins hung from the walls alongside framed photographs of skinny African women with silver coils wrapped tightly around their elongated necks.

"Those aren't Ethiopian women," you said, gesturing with your chin toward the photographs. "They're from the Zatusi tribe. They live in Kenya, mostly."

Our mutual friend Michael, the birthday boy, stood swaying at the far end of the table, glass of wine in hand, and declared: "I am thirty years old, goddamnit, and I'm not happy about it." But I couldn't listen to Michael.

"Were you with him when he died?" I asked.

"I was holding his hand. He looked like a fresh-hatched chick."

"The main things is," said Michael, "the main *thing*, I mean, is that all my best friends are here tonight. Except for *you*," he said, pointing at me. "Who the hell are you?"

I got nervous for a second but then everybody started laughing and I laughed, too. You laughed, and then you squeezed my knee under the table.

"Just kidding, Frankie," said Michael. "We're all glad you could make it tonight. Later on Frankie's going to entertain us with the opening chapters of his dissertation on John Donne's Holy Sonnets. So we've got that to look forward to." The annoying thing is that Michael was an English major in college; he can skillfully mock my profession. Michael runs his own hedge fund; I have no idea what that means. He pays for dinner, that's what it means.

Once I was sure that Michael had finished with me, I asked you what you meant by a new-hatched chick. You had moved your seat closer to mine; I could smell your perfume now. Cinnamon.

"Have you ever seen a chick coming out of its shell?" you asked me. "It's just this fuzzed head bobbing on a skinny, skinny body. That's what Leonard looked like. My dad. He only weighed about a hundred pounds when he died."

"Was he in a lot of pain?"

"He was so out of it. I don't know. I hope not. It's like when you catch a spider in a jar, and you screw the top on tight, and at first he's in there scooting all over the place, but then he starts running out of air, he gets slower and slower, and finally he just topples over."

I was thinking about that for a while.

"It was hard seeing him get so small," you told me. "He used to be a big guy, a really big guy. He was in a motorcycle gang in the sixties."

"Really? The Hell's Angels?"

"The Suicide Kings. They were a lot tougher than the Hell's Angels. When the Suicide Kings walked into a bar, the Hell's Angels just finished their drinks and left. Did you ever read the Hunter Thompson book about the Hell's Angels?"

"No."

"Leonard's in that book. He once hit a guy so hard he broke his hand, and when he was in the hospital getting the bone set, the doctors found the guy's tooth. It was buried between two knuckles."

"The guy's tooth?"

"Can you imagine that? The tooth was buried like an inch deep."

"That's a good punch." I ran my tongue over my own teeth. "The guy he punched was a Hell's Angel?"

"No. He was a marine biologist."

"When you turn thirty," said Michael from the head of the table, "it really makes you sit back and take stock of your life. So I did and the next day the bottom fell out of the market and now I'm selling at seven and one quarter." The room went loud with laughter, all of Michael's financial friends banging the tabletop and howling. I put on my grin, feeling like an idiot.

"Poor Michael," you said. "He used to be so charming."

I wanted you so badly my stomach hurt: your pale face framed in wild tangles of near-black hair, your small and crooked teeth, your collarbone a quick sketch of wings. Forgive me for saying this, but your beauty is strange, and I was proud to discover it, proud of my eye, like a record-store clerk who proudly wears the black T-shirt of his beloved, unsigned band.

"It took him two hours to burn."

There was violence between my thoughts and your words. I decided I had heard you wrong. "I'm sorry, what?"

"Leonard. He was so skinny by the time he died. It's the fat that burns hottest. They said it took him two hours to burn to ashes."

"They told you that?"

"Usually it's an hour, hour and a half. You wouldn't think it would take so long."

"I guess I never really thought about it."

"It's the bones," you said, pushing your chair back from the table and standing up. "Bones take a long time to burn. It was nice meeting you, Frankie."

"You're going?"

"I have to. A friend of mine is playing the Blue Note tonight. Get my number from Michael," you told me, bending down to kiss my cheek. I tried to return the kiss but you had already turned away. I sat at the table and watched the crooked candles burn, while everyone around me drank and laughed and ended up singing "American Pie."

· · ·

I got your number from Michael and called you the next night, but you were busy that week, and busy the week after, and I resigned myself to never seeing you again. But then you called me, one month after the birthday party, and invited me to watch the meteor shower.

"It's supposed to be best right after sunset," you told me. "Meet me in the Sheep Meadow."

The sun was nearly down. I brushed my teeth while showering and the sky was still bright as I climbed down the stairs to my subway station. Thirty minutes later I was stumbling over angry meteor-watchers in the Sheep Meadow. I had forgotten to ask you where to meet, and the Meadow is huge, especially on a moonless night. I thought I saw you lying belly-down on a blanket and I leaned close to make sure.

"Back off, fuck-face," said a teenage girl.

Finally I heard you calling my name. "Frankie," you called. "Hey! Frankie! Over here, cutie."

You sat cross-legged on a quilt, dressed in black. All I could see were your hands and face, and the white smoke rising from your mouth. "Take a seat," you said, patting the place beside you. "Take a seat and a smoke." You handed me a tightly rolled joint and I sat down with it, inhaling deeply.

"Sorry I'm late," I said. "I couldn't find you."

"I know. I've been watching you wander around." You laughed. "I'm sorry, I know it's mean. But you looked so cute, so sad. Like a lost puppy."

"Oh" is what I said.

"You're not mad at me, are you?" you asked, taking the joint back.

"Nope." I really wasn't. It never occurred to me that I should be mad. I was sitting with you on a quilt in the darkness. Everything was good.

"You know what I love about you, Frankie?"

I shook my head.

"You don't have a mean bone in your body."

I said nothing, but it seemed to me like a weak motive for love. You bent toward me and I saw a flash of crooked teeth before you bit me hard on the lips. We lay back to watch the sky, passing the joint back and forth. It was August and the air was warm, the grass thick and soft below our quilt. I felt the smoke curling through my body, rounding the corners as it went. You blew a ring of smoke above our heads, and we watched it grow larger and larger until the dark swallowed it.

"Look," you said, pointing with a pale finger. "Shooting star."

I squinted but saw nothing. "I missed it."

"There's another one."

We smoked and talked about movies and rated the buildings of Central Park South, but every time a meteor blazed by I was looking the wrong way.

"I wish you could have met Leonard," you told me. "My dad. He would've liked you."

. . .

That very first night you took me home with you, but nobody got naked. The minute I walked in the door I began sneezing. Your twin black cats sat in the windowsill and stared at me with bored, yellow eyes. I stared back at them while you stepped into the kitchen alcove and boiled water for tea. When the kettle began to whistle both cats raised their right paws and clawed at the air. They watched me to see what I would do. I blinked and turned away.

"Your cats are kind of scary."

"They *are* scary. The cross-eyed one, Luther, he understands Portuguese. Are you allergic?"

"No," I lied.

Most of your apartment was bed, a giant bed with wrought-iron headboard and footboard. A small wooden desk, holding a blue ceramic lamp and a spiral notebook, crouched bowlegged in one corner. Your apartment was on the twentieth floor, but all you could see through the windows were the twentieth-floor apartments across the street.

"Here," you said, handing me a cup of tea, "ginseng." We sat on the giant bed and blew on our tea. "This bed used to be Leonard's. I mean, a while ago. I've had it for years. At his funeral I met all these women, his old lovers. And every one I met, all I could think was: Did they do it on my bed? I've been getting these letters from people, all these friends of Leonard's, people from all over the country. One guy from Australia."

I sneezed.

"These letters—nobody who met my dad forgot him. I get letters from people who met him *one* time; I got a letter from this woman who *never* even met him, but her husband always used to talk about him. God, Frankie, you should see these letters." You stared at your cross-eyed cat. "People loved Leonard." We were quiet for a while and then you said, "Here, I'll show you one." You gave me your teacup to hold and went over to your little bowlegged desk. "But you have to promise not to ask who wrote it, okay?"

"Sure."

You pulled a sheet of folded paper from the desk drawer and brought it over to me. "Read this part," you said, sitting beside me, underlining the sentences with your finger. The letter was typed and unsigned. The part I read:

When he was sober he was the most courteous man alive, a true gentleman. He remembered everybody's birthdays and anniversaries and would always send flowers, always chrysanthemums. A man from the old school, opening car doors for ladies, standing everyone drinks when he was flush. He was a saint, your father. He'd steal the pennies from a dead man's eyes, but he was a saint.

You folded the paper neatly and returned it to the desk drawer. "You wouldn't believe me if I told you who wrote that."

"Of course I would." I scrunched up my eyes and tried to prevent another sneeze.

You picked up a book from the desktop and handed it to me, taking the teacups in exchange and resting them on a wicker nightstand. "He had this with him by his hospital bed. He read it every day. At the very end, when he went blind, I read to him."

I held the battered blue hardcover in my hands, the pages worn from being turned too often, blue loops of illegible script in the margins, paper clips marking the crucial passages.

"*Moby-Dick*? I thought he was more of an *On the Road* guy."

You shook your head violently. "He thought Kerouac was a fraud. But *Moby-Dick*, God, he loved that book. There's this one part he knew by heart . . ." You took the book from me and paged through it. "Here," you said, pointing to two sentences boxed in blue ink, three blue stars in the margin.

I bent forward to read the lines and then smiled. "That was my professor's favorite part, too."

"Leonard would just say it to himself. He'd repeat it over and over. He rode out of the Catskills when he was sixteen and never went back, but he was always a kid from the mountains. And that quote," you said, tapping the printed words with an unpainted fingernail, "it was like his mantra."

"It's beautiful," I said. I sneezed again.

You nodded, running your fingers over the groove of blue ink. You closed the book and handed it back to me. "I want you to have it."

"Wait—"

"Take it, Frankie. Maybe you'll teach Melville someday and you can use Leonard's notes."

I wanted to tell you that my field was literature of England, sixteenth and seventeenth centuries, that I would never teach a course in *Moby-Dick*, that, more importantly, I had not earned a gift this great, but you had already left the bed. You knelt down by a blue milk crate stacked with record sleeves.

"Here he is," you told me, your hand on a large black jar with a brass lid resting on a stereo amplifier.

I opened my mouth and then closed it. I looked over at the cats and they were both staring at me, cross-eyed Luther flicking his tail. I looked back at you and the black jar and said, "Leonard?"

"Uh huh. It's not really an official urn. I thought a real urn would look morbid."

I bet some people would think keeping pop in a black jar above the amplifier was morbid, but I didn't say that. Instead I said, "Weren't you going to scatter him in that reservoir?"

"The Neversink. Yeah, but Frankie, the state doesn't really like people throwing their daddy's ashes in the drinking water. Leonard was the outlaw, not me."

. . .

Two days later you told me I was your boyfriend and we made love to prove it. Leonard's bed was covered in black cat hair and my entire body broke out in hives. My eyes were so swollen I could barely see. Both nostrils were clogged shut; I lay on my back sucking in air while Luther and the other cat, whose name I never learned, sat on the windowsill and stared at me.

"Maybe we should go to your place," you suggested.

"If you want," I said.

You ended up loving my apartment for its view of the Manhattan skyline. "This is so *good*. I can't wait till it rains. I want to see the Empire State Building in the rain. Or the snow! I can't wait till it snows."

We brought a suitcase full of your clothes to my apartment, and a shopping bag filled with your other necessities. Favorite albums, essential spices, toiletries, refrigerator magnets, an ebony hand-mirror that had belonged to your grandmother, a one-armed G.I. Joe doll that five-year-old Leonard had found beneath the Christmas tree.

"I'll go back there every couple of days," you told me. "And check on the cats. I hope they'll be all right without me."

I nodded. "I really hope so."

One night I woke up thirsty and reached for a glass of water on the bedside table. You were awake, your back against the headboard, staring out the window at glittering Manhattan in the distance.

"It's so beautiful, Frankie."

"I know."

You said nothing else. I drank my water and curled up again to sleep. And then you asked, "Do you know who wrote that letter?"

I opened my eyes. "What letter?"

"The letter I read you, the one about Leonard. About sending the chrysanthemums and stealing the pennies?"

"No, who wrote it?"

You watched the city, your eyes unblinking. "Frank Sinatra."

. . .

We were together for nine months, and then we weren't together. One day I was your "cutie" and the next day I was "still your best friend"; it took me a while to figure out that a cutie is superior to a best friend, that a cutie gets to live with you and make love to you, while a best friend gets sympathetic cheek-kisses and long, meaningful hugs.

You packed your suitcase and abandoned the view of Manhattan, returned to Luther and his nameless brother, to Leonard's ashes and Leonard's bed.

"Do you want *Moby-Dick* back?" I asked, as you folded your sweaters.

"You keep it. Maybe someday you'll teach a class on Melville."

I held the door open for you and you stood in the hallway, suitcase in one hand, shopping bag in the other. "You know I love you, don't you, Frankie?"

"Sure," I said. "It's pretty obvious."

You shook your head sadly and kissed me on the cheek. "Sarcasm does not become you."

"Sorry," I said.

The day after you left me for good my face erupted with the worst case of acne I'd had since high school. I woke up in the morning to the familiar sensation, something ticking in the space between my eyebrows. In the bathroom mirror I saw my fears confirmed. An angry red pimple glared back; that's the way it always starts for me.

The day after you left me was a Sunday. I had nothing to do but sit on my candy-striped sofa and pretend to read. Pretending to read is one of my talents; I'm making a career of it. Eventually I'll earn my doctorate and teach students who pretend to read.

Every few hours I carefully marked my page and went to the bathroom to check the mirror, morbidly fascinated by the progressive ruin of my face. I wondered if my true skin would ever reemerge. Or if this *was* my true skin, this troubled terrain, and the face of the last ten years a dream of perfect pores.

A tube of prescription ointment lay waiting in the medicine cabinet, but I decided to go without. The treatment never worked, but more than that, I felt this punishment must be just, my own plague of boils.

The things you forgot to pack: a bottle of rum-soaked vanilla beans on the cupboard shelf, an orange toothbrush on the edge of the sink, and a spare pair of keys to your apartment.

I stared at the vanilla beans for a long time. I thought they were the saddest things I'd ever seen, the skinny corpses of a family caught in a house fire, charred beyond recognition. The toothbrush I threw out the window, watched it cartwheel down, watched it lodge in the blooming branches of a dogwood tree. It's still there, that toothbrush, an orange fuck-you finger pointing at me whenever I walk past the tree.

My mind was filled with your stories. And especially with Leonard. God, I loved listening to you talk. We'd stay up late, huddled in our cold bed, a slumber party for two, the arthritic radiator groaning from the corner of the room. And you would tell me stories. Your family was filled with rowdy drunks: card-sharps, bigamists, saxophonists, and lion-trainers. All of them insane and all of them full-color. You were the first woman I'd ever met who told family stories that I wanted to hear. I couldn't get enough. And I would feel guilty that I couldn't tell you any beauties in return. The drunks I know are quiet drunks, tight-mouthed and scab-knuckled. They scared me out of my hometown.

But Leonard, Leonard, I can't get him out of my mind. He was the hero of all your greatest tales: half-mad, a famous lover of women, still invoked reverentially in certain downtown taverns for heroic benders that lasted three days. I never met the man but I can't get him out of my mind.

When Monday morning came I was still lying on the sofa, my throat and forehead graveled with red pustules, the unread book waiting quietly on my belly. Manhattan loomed pale blue across the river until the sun rose behind me, igniting the eastern-aspect windows. You were over there, on that crowded island, sleeping in Leonard's bed. I narrowed my eyes and rendered all the concrete and steel and glass invisible, disappeared the water towers and television antennae, until all there was to see of the city was column upon column of sleepers, in pajamas, in boxer shorts, in nightgowns, naked. Millions of dreaming New Yorkers, dreaming of faithless husbands and faceless lovers, a sky raining fat girls, dragons nestled in the nave of the Cathedral of Saint John the Divine. And you, you dreamed on with them, about heaven knows what, floating twenty stories above the avenue.

Finally I pushed myself off the candy-striped sofa, staggered into the kitchen, and began grinding beans for coffee. When I had a pot brewing I picked up the phone and called Michael. He's always at his office before six in the morning, reading the business sections of newspapers from around the world. He picked up on the first ring and I told him I needed to borrow his car that night so I could attend an MLA conference up at SUNY Binghamton.

"Sounds like a blast," he said. "What's the topic?"

I stared at the blank face of my refrigerator. You had taken all your magnets home with you. "It's a literary conference," I said.

"Right, but there's got to be a topic. Fart Jokes of the Kalahari Bushmen—something like that?"

"I wish. This one is Captivity Narratives of the Post-Colonial Americas."

He whistled. "You're going to bring Pocahontas back in the trunk?"

"So it's okay?"

"What happened, you found out about this conference today?"

"My ride fell through. I was going to take a bus but—"

"It's kind of weird that they scheduled the conference for a Tuesday, isn't it?"

"It is," I said. "It's really weird."

"What I don't get—" he began, but I cut him off.

"Here's the thing, Michael, please don't fuck with me right now."

I sensed him grinning, the Frankfurt morning paper splashed across his desk. "All right," he said. "I'll let the garage guy know you're coming."

• • •

That evening I called your apartment from a pay phone on your corner; when you answered I hung up. This is what I've become, I told myself: a creep who calls his ex-girlfriend and hangs up. I waited in the coffee shop across the street from your building, hoping that you would emerge before too long. Too long passed and the pretty waitress grew tired of refilling my bottomless cup; she sat at the counter and ignored me. I stared out the window and played with the salt-shaker and studied my infested face in the hollow of a spoon. Finally I saw you walk out of your building. You were alone and I thanked you for that small mercy.

I crossed the street and unlocked the front door and the vestibule door with your spare keys, rode the elevator to the twentieth floor, and entered your apartment. The two black cats lay on the bed, unsurprised to see me. "Hello, Luther," I said to the cross-eyed cat. I nodded to the other cat. "Hello," I said, embarrassed not to know his name.

I lifted the heavy black jar of Leonard's ashes from the amplifier and turned to leave. The cats watched me. "*Ladrão*," I said to Luther, pointing my thumb at myself. That means "thief" in Portuguese, but Luther gave no sign that he cared. My eyes watering, I waved farewell to the cats and walked out of the apartment.

It was a long ride crosstown to Michael's garage. I sat in the back of a city bus, half-stoned on diesel fumes, the black jar resting on my lap. Nobody noticed the urn that was not an urn. I wanted to elbow the old man sitting next to me, an old man chewing the stub of a pencil, holding a folded newspaper inches from his eyes, studying the crossword puzzle. I wanted to nudge him and say, "These are the ashes of my ex-girlfriend's father. This is all that remains of an American original. Would you like to pay your respects?"

We made our way eastward, the engine grumbling below my seat, the city outside lit yellow by streetlamps, the pedestrians trudging forward with bowed heads, the store owners standing on the sidewalk, smoking cigarettes and lowering the steel shutters. And Leonard nothing but the loot of a pimpled thief.

. . .

I drove Michael's race car back to Brooklyn with me. Every hour I would look down from my window to make sure it was still where I parked it. The car was too red for my street, too shiny.

I studied the maps and plotted my route, and at six in the morning, after dozing for three hours, I went down to the beautiful car. I was afraid the urn would burst open if I left it in the trunk, so I strapped it into the passenger seat, alongside the broken-spined copy of *Moby-Dick*, and drove carefully, slow on the turns. We crossed the Brooklyn Bridge into Manhattan, up the West Side Highway, over the George Washington Bridge into New Jersey, north on the Garden State Parkway before crossing back into New York. A two-hour drive to Sullivan County, the radio tuned to an oldies station that serenaded us with Carl Perkins and Elvis Presley, Jerry Lee Lewis and Bill Monroe, Southern voices heavy with bullying sexuality fried in bacon fat. The sun rose over an unseen Atlantic, the highways unspooled and the radio played on, crackling with needled vinyl. And that morning it seemed to me that love is a singer, Brylcreamed and mutton-chopped, bad mannered, snarling into the microphone with a voice cigarette-blasted, a voice addled by cheap whiskey. But he can hit the high notes, and he can hit the low.

Leonard was a good man for the shotgun seat. Not that we communicated, I don't mean that. I mean that memories of Leonard crowded my mind. Your memories of Leonard. He refused to be photographed, you told me; he was deeply superstitious, believed with the Bedouins that a photograph was a trap for the soul. I never saw his face. But I pictured him fierce-eyed and blue-jawed, thick eyebrows tilting as he leans forward to make a joke. I pictured him a long-limbed Napoleon, strutting about the shores of Elba, an emperor in exile.

And I pictured him drunk. You told me he swallowed his first glass of whiskey in the morning, before eating his scrambled eggs and blood pudding. But Leonard's drinking, save for the legendary benders, was workmanlike, and his tolerance astounding.

"Did I ever tell you about Leonard and Gloria Steinem?" you asked me one night, lying in bed, as I kissed your belly. Leonard decided in 1973 that he wanted to understand what the feminists were all about. He went to hear a speech Steinem was giving at an auditorium in Chicago. All through the talk, on equity in the workplace, on proposals for legally enforced maternity leaves, Leonard guzzled from his bottle of Old Grand-Dad, ignoring the angry looks of the women sitting beside him. Finally he lurched to his feet, dropping his empty bottle to the floor. It rolled loudly down the aisle. Faces turned to look at him.

"You are a beautiful woman," he declared. Steinem raised her famous eyebrows. "You are a beautiful woman," he repeated, and the crowd began to hiss. "I love you," he said, above the hisses. "I love you, Ms. Steinem."

We made good time, arriving in the town of Liberty before eight. I bought an apple and a Wing Ding and a Coke at the only store open, a dusty corner market, got directions to the reservoir from the checkout girl. Her face was awash in small red pimples, and I smiled at her, pointed at my own agitated skin, and said, "The humidity, right?" But she frowned and turned away.

I ate breakfast sitting on the hood of Michael's car. A strong wind blew through the town; wax-paper cups and coupon flyers and tinfoil wrappers paraded down the empty street, leaping and tumbling for my enjoyment. Back in the car I checked my face in the vanity mirror; my lips were smudged with chocolate. That will do wonders for my complexion, I thought. I turned the ignition on and then immediately off. I walked back into the market and bought the heaviest chocolate bar I could find. I could tell the girl thought it was a bad idea; she counted out my change angrily and slapped it into my palm. I returned to the car, unwrapped the chocolate, and ate the whole thing in four bites. "Fuck it," I said, patting Leonard's urn. "Right?"

The checkout girl's directions were precise; fifteen minutes later we were bouncing over a dirt road and I switched to a country station. I winced at each pebble cracking against the car's underbody. We crested a small hill and I saw a chain-link fence rising from the grass ahead, black-and-red No Trespassing signs hanging at regular intervals. I looked at Leonard's urn, half-expecting a reaction, some excitement for this homecoming.

Breaking into a reservoir is disturbingly easy. The chain-link fence was only eight feet high, with no barbed wire on top. No security guards patrolled the perimeter with leashed Dobermans. No surveillance cameras. No motion detectors.

I slipped *Moby-Dick* under my waistband, unbuckled Leonard's urn and carried him over to the fence. It occurred to me that most of the man had already been released, that of his living two hundred pounds only four remained, the rest escaped as smoke through the crematorium chimney. Our bodies are mostly water, I remembered. This was Leonard's essence here, the unburnable, the pit of the man.

I stood before the fence with the urn cradled in my palms. Climbing over would be easy, but not while carrying the urn. An athlete could do it, Michael could do it, but not me. Throwing the urn over the fence was not an option. The whole point of this journey was to transport Leonard to his chosen resting place with the dignity he deserved. What if the urn cracked open, spilling his ashes over the grass?

I rotated the problem in my mind for several minutes, then placed the urn carefully at the foot of the fence, walked over to the car and opened the trunk. And luck was with me: a pair of black bungee cords lay waiting, used by Michael to strap bulky objects to the roof. I fastened the urn to the small of my back with a cord wrapped around twice and hooked tight at the waist. I was very proud of my improvisation and stood there for a moment with my hands on my hips. Then I clambered up the fence. At the very top, as I turned around and prepared to descend to the other side, the urn came loose and fell to the ground. I climbed down quickly and snatched it from the dirt, ashamed of my clumsiness, and inspected it for damage. No cracks at all, only a price sticker on the bottom. *Pottery Barn*, it read, *$29.95.*

I couldn't believe you had left the price-sticker on Leonard's urn. But then I berated myself for meanness; you bought the urn days after your father's death. How could I expect you to remember the social niceties? I peeled the sticker off with my thumbnail and watched the wind blow it into the woods.

The Neversink itself was a disappointment. I had expected a mighty man-made lake, the far shore hazed by distance, but the actual reservoir was small and only half-full, the lower terraces of the concrete embankment shaded dark where they had recently been immersed. It seemed to me that if every citizen of New York's five boroughs flushed their toilet at the exact same time, the Neversink would empty down its drain with a great and final gasp.

Each terrace of the embankment sloped to a step five feet high; I jumped seven of them, convinced every time that I would shatter my ankle. But my ankle held and I reached the last terrace, after which the concrete plunged thirty feet vertically before hitting the water. The wind was at my back and I decided here was the right place.

Resting the urn on the step above mine, I drew *Moby-Dick* from my jeans' waistband and thumbed through the paper-clipped pages, looking for Leonard's mantra. There it was, marked with three blue stars. I cleared my throat and read. *"There is a wisdom that is woe; but there is a woe that is madness. And there is a Catskill eagle in some souls that can alike dive down into the blackest gorges, and soar out of them again and become invisible in the sunny spaces."*

I stared into the blue water below. "You don't know me,

Leonard, but I've heard a lot about you. I wish we could have met one time; I wish I could have bought you a drink. And I know you can't hear me, I know you're dead and all that, but I want you to know that I love your daughter. I wish you were alive so I could come ask for your blessing."

I jammed the book into my waistband and began trying to pry the lid off the urn. For a second I feared it was hopelessly stuck, but I used the car key and managed to pop it free. I closed my eyes. I had read that human ashes were rarely pure ash, that knucklebones and splinters of skull and fire-blackened curls of femur were mixed in like shells in a bucket of sand. What I held in my hands was a pot of burned man. The only sounds I could hear were the wind, blowing against my body, blowing over the Neversink waters, and a big machine's low humming from somewhere far away. I reached into the urn and my fingers touched paper. I opened my eyes. I looked inside—a yellow paper sack. I returned the jar to the step above mine and tugged out the sack. *Gold Medal Flour*, read the writing on the yellow paper. *America's #1 Bread Flour*. I stood in the wind for a long time, reading those words. Maybe he's inside, I thought. Maybe Leonard is packed in there, to keep him from spilling all over the place. I unfolded the top of the sack and reached in for a handful. What my hand held was white flour.

The humming was louder now. High overhead a propeller plane unzipped the morning sky. I walked to the edge of the terrace, reached my hand out over the reservoir and let the flour sift through my fingers. The wind made a fast cloud of it. I emptied the entire bag of Gold Medal, watched the falling flour expand and expand until by the time it hit the water it had no more substance than dandelion fur.

· · ·

I called you the next night. "Hello," I said. "It's Frankie."

"Hello, Frankie. God, you sound so formal."

"I read the Hunter Thompson book," I told you. *"Hell's Angels."*

"Oh, really? Hold on a second." I pictured your hand covering the receiver, muffling the voices I heard, the laughter. "Hey."

"Hey."

"So you liked it?" you asked.

"Yes. But the thing is, Leonard's not in it."

"The top shelf."

I squinted. "The top shelf? What does that mean?"

"No, I wasn't talking to you."

"I read the book because you said Leonard was in it."

"He *is* in it."

"No," I said. "I read the whole book. He's not in it."

"Well, he didn't go by his *real* name when he was in the gang. What do you think, everyone called him Leonard? He had some code name."

"Oh. So, did you notice he's not in your living room anymore?"

"What?" I pictured you looking at your amplifier, realizing for the first time that the fake urn was missing. "Where is it? You came in here?"

"Yes."

"You broke into my apartment?" You laughed. "Wow, Frankie, that's a little scary."

"I stole Leonard. You know why? I stole Leonard and I brought him up to the Catskills."

There was silence on the line for a moment. In the background I heard someone hammering a nail into the wall. Then you said: "Frankie—"

"I brought him to the Neversink, and I read his favorite Melville passage, and I opened the urn."

"I can't believe this."

"Why did you do that to me?" I asked.

"I can't believe you're accusing me. You come in here and rob my apartment, and then you accuse *me*? I trust you with my key and you rob me, and now, now you're *accusing* me?"

"I just want to know—"

"Okay, you want to know? My father lives in Pasadena. I haven't seen him in nine years. Now you know. Happy? Anything else? You want his name?"

"Pasadena?"

"Pasadena. He's a tax attorney. Okay? Happy now?"

"There's no Leonard?" I asked.

"There's no Frankie," you answered, and hung up the phone.

. . .

Every time I look out my window I see the city where you live, and I wonder where you are, and what you're doing, hidden behind the stacks of tall buildings. Nothing so mundane as laundry or grocery shopping—no, the laws of bad reality don't apply to you, you give birth to dead fathers.

Somewhere in the city Leonard exists, haunting the mind of another blessed suitor. I'm in mourning for a man who never was, that's true, but I still expect to meet Leonard one day, playing dice in the backroom of a sawdust bar, a crude mermaid tattooed on his forearm, a battered copy of *Moby-Dick* in the pocket of his leather jacket. I'll buy him a glass of whiskey and listen to his stories.

MERDE FOR LUCK

1

The woman in the window seat is the first to notice the stink. She begins to frown even before she raises her eyes from her paperback novel. She flares her nostrils and squints; then, when she realizes that the smell is not going away, she closes her book and turns to look at me. She wants to know if I smell it, too. I don't give her the satisfaction. I stare at the bald head in front of me.

The other passengers nearby are becoming aware that something is wrong. They turn in their seats and look about the cabin; they grimace at each other; they fan the air with newspapers and magazines. A stewardess, her black hair knotted in an immaculate chignon, walks slowly down the aisle, sniffing with her nose raised, a bird dog flushing pheasant. She stops two rows in front of me and bends down beside a young mother holding a sleeping infant. The stewardess whispers a question and the mother shakes her head, smiling.

"Clean that baby," snaps an old woman sitting behind me. "If they want to take a baby on board," she tells her husband loudly, "they ought to have the decency to keep it clean."

"It's not the baby," says the stewardess, straightening up and continuing to walk toward the rear of the plane. When she reaches my row she pauses, looks first to her left and then to her right, and her eyes fix on me. The dark stain spreads below me on the seat cushion, out of sight, but the stewardess doesn't need to see the evidence—she smells it on me, smells my guilt. She walks a few rows farther to verify that I am the source of the trouble. The woman in the window seat already knows. She presses herself as close to the cabin wall as she can, stares at me with confusion and disgust.

The stewardess returns and crouches next to me. "Sir," she asks, "are you feeling ill?"

"No," I tell her.

She keeps her voice low, to protect me from embarrassment, to keep the situation calm. "Have you had an accident?" she asks.

I do not look at her. The bald man in front of me has turned to watch. He looks like my grandfather, a white mustache above a kind mouth, his ears outstretched like the wings of a swan rising from a lake.

"Sir," repeats the stewardess, "if you're feeling sick, I can help you. This happens sometimes, it's nothing to worry about."

I say nothing.

"We can get you into a change of clothes, give you something to settle your stomach. Do you want to come with me?"

"No."

The man who is not my grandfather shakes his head at

the stewardess. The look he gives her says: *We're dealing with a crazy.*

The stewardess tries one more time. "Why don't we go to the back of the plane, sir. I really think you'll feel better." When I fail to respond she sighs and stands, smooths out the wrinkles in her pleated blue skirt, and walks quickly to the front of the cabin.

Some of the passengers have left their seats; they stand in small groups at a safe distance, whispering and giggling and staring at me. I don't look at them. I don't try to hear what they are saying. I sit in my own shit and wait.

The stewardess returns with another member of the crew, a handsome boy with a dimpled chin and carefully molded forelock. "Is there anything we can do to help you, sir?" he asks.

"No."

"All right," he says, quickly dropping the air of supplication. "I'm going to have to ask you to come with us. Please, sir, let's not make this difficult."

I buckle my seat belt and pull the strap tight.

The steward and the stewardess exchange glances. *Why this? Why now?* I watch them from the corner of my eye, prepared to resist should they put their hands on me. But we haven't gotten to that stage yet. They have no desire to use physical force. They did not ask for this problem; they did not want this to happen. I understand that. I didn't want it to happen either. I have never been a troublemaker. Until now. These people need to be troubled.

"I have to warn you, sir," says the steward, "causing a disturbance on an interstate flight is a federal offense."

He waits for a response. There is no response.

"I'm going to repeat," says the steward. "I'm repeating this one time. We need you to come with us to the back of the plane. Otherwise we'll call the airport and have officers waiting there when we touch down. Okay? Sir, do you understand what I'm saying?"

"He's sick," whispers the stewardess. She rests her hand on my shoulder. "Sir, please. We'll get you cleaned up and into some dry clothes."

"I need to get out of here," says the woman in the window seat. "This is insane. He's making *me* sick."

"Get Jimmy," the steward tells the stewardess. "We need to move this guy."

I want them to understand. I want to show them what happened. If I pulled his photograph from my wallet, let them see his smile, his head tilted back in mid-laugh, would that work? Would they nod and bite their lips, grip my shoulder in solidarity? Or would they hiss?

2

His name was not Hector, but that's what I'll call him. I met him in a penthouse apartment far above the city streets. The man who owned the place, a famous photographer whose images of pretty boys and girls stood seven stories high in Times Square, had called me that afternoon to invite me to the party. I guessed I was replacing a more glamorous guest, a late cancellation.

"Bring a razor," the photographer told me. "I'll supply the rest."

A servant, hired for the evening, met me at the door and helped me out of my raincoat. I've had that job before; I've catered rich people's parties, poured their drinks and bused their dishes. I almost told him that, but I realized the intended gesture of sympathy would come across as merely patronizing—*I used to do menial work, too. And now look at me!*

The living room was empty. I panicked for a moment, the old high school chill, suspected that the entire party was a ruse. Lure Alexander here with promises, let him think he will play with the popular kids, while the real party rages miles away, the revelers laughing as they picture my confusion. But a pale-faced girl wearing a tuxedo stood behind a white-clothed table topped with rows of bottled liquor. I accepted a glass of vodka and looked around the room. The photographer's famous subjects hung from the walls, glassed and framed, smiling their famous smiles. I sipped my vodka and studied their poses. Stars, all of them, but they couldn't compete with the view out the windows, everything blurred and spectral in the rain, headlights and taillights streaming along the avenues, distant bridges glimmering like pearls for Godzilla—my nighttime city.

I thought I would rather look out the rain-pelted glass than at anything else, but I was wrong.

"Are you Alexander?"

I turned around. A naked man, wet from the shower, holding a rolled towel in one hand, stood on the silver carpet. I looked at the girl behind the bar but she pretended to fidget with a corkscrew.

"Yes," I said. I stared down at my rain boots, my olive

green wide-wale corduroys, my black cashmere turtleneck sweater. "I feel overdressed."

He nodded, half-smiling. He had the most perfect body I'd ever seen. The water did not want to run off his skin—it beaded on him, like drops on the hood of a freshly waxed car.

"We've been waiting for you. Come on, follow me."

This is why I came to the city, I thought. So that beautiful, naked men could say: *We've been waiting for you. Come on, follow me.* Anywhere, sir, I thought to myself, draining the rest of the vodka.

The room we entered must have been the photographer's studio. The radiators were cranking and the air was lush, tropical. A giant white tarp had been laid across the center of the floor. Blue buckets of steaming water sat on the tarp; yellow sponges floated on the water. Twelve men stood naked on the tarp, holding drinks, chatting and laughing and whispering into one another's ears. Thirteen men stood naked on the tarp when my guide had joined them. It was 1991, before the rage for tattoos and piercings; everyone's skin was their own. I recognized six or seven faces, well-known artists and art writers.

"Alexander!" cried the photographer. "At last! A party of thirteen is a very nasty omen. We would have had to kill someone! Alexander, everyone. Everyone, Alexander."

"Hello, Alexander," the friendlier ones chorused. The others simply glanced at me and resumed their conversations.

"Alexander is a *very* talented young sculptor," the photographer continued, already losing interest in me.

"Painter," I said.

"Now," said the photographer. "Who first?"

"Me," said my guide. "I'm freezing."

"Nobody told you to take a shower," said a tall, lanky man wearing square black glasses, a critic for one of the city's glossy magazines. "You just wanted to preempt us with the wet and wild look."

"Fine," said the photographer, "fine. Hector is first. Pick a man, Hector, pick a man! Whom do you choose?"

Hector stared directly at me, his brown eyes framed by long lashes. A thrill of desire shivered me in my boots.

"Him. Alexander."

The photographer raised his eyebrows. "To the latecomer go the spoils. There you go, Alexander. Welcome to the party. Come, join us. Sans the clothes."

I placed my glass on the floor and stripped nervously, conscious of the watching eyes, stumbling on one foot as I pried off my boots. I'm not badly built—I ran the marathon that year—but Hector, well, Hector's body was a gift, a miracle. People are not meant to look that good. It's not healthy for society.

I stepped onto the tarp, conscious of the silence. My mind was crazed with curiosity, and shyness, and most of all, desire.

"Your razor," whispered the photographer. "Where's your razor?"

I jogged back to my clothes and pulled the leather case from my pants' pocket. On the tarp I unzipped the case, removed the tortoiseshell handle inside, and opened the steel blade.

"Uh oh," said someone in the crowd. A low, nervous laughter rose up from them.

"Do you know how to use that?" asked the critic.

"Yes," I told him. I did. My father swore by the straight-edge, insisted that safety razors were for pansies and pubescent girls. He taught me the technique before I had any whiskers of my own.

Hector smiled. I had expected his teeth to be perfect, and they were, so white his face grew darker against them. "Come on," he said, "I trust you."

I knew the rules of the game. He stood waiting for me, his feet apart, hands on his hips. Already he was growing aroused and I knew it wasn't me. He was on display. All eyes watched him; everyone in the room wanted him.

I carried a blue bucket over to him, dipped a yellow sponge wrist-deep into the soapy water and then circled Hector the way I would circle a marble statue in the museum, inspecting him, front, flanks, and rear. Standing behind him, razor handle in my mouth like a pirate, I wrung out the sponge, watched the water cascade down his back, down the steep channel of his spine, through the cleft of his buttocks and down his legs before puddling at his feet. Hector was rocking gently back and forth, pressing himself against me and away, a sly, teasing motion.

I thought of the first boy I had fucked, a quiet punk rocker with spiked orange hair. We thought it would be funny to screw each other in the end zone of our high school football field, and it was, we were laughing hysterically as we tore each other nude. But then he grew abruptly silent, turned away on all fours, and offered himself to me. It was Saturday night, the school's lights all out, the crickets screaming, the wind rattling the pine branches. Stars everywhere, hovering above the hilltops, above the school's clock tower, above our own steaming skin.

But this was part of Hector's game. He wanted me to forget myself, to drop the razor and *do him*, here and now, standing on the wet tarp. I don't think our audience would have complained; they stared at us feverishly, waiting.

I dropped to my knees and lathered the twin-veined diamonds of Hector's calves. He stood on the balls of his feet, to flex the muscle, and it struck me how intimately Hector knew his own body, far better than I knew my own. He knew exactly how to stand, how to move, where to place his hands. He knew what rippled when he stretched his arms. Hector, I understood, enjoyed a lifelong affair with mirrors.

"Aren't you afraid?" he asked, looking down at me, his chin resting on his shoulder, his tone lightly mocking. "Shouldn't you wear gloves?"

"I'm not going to cut you."

I rested the sponge on the tarp and began shaving him. Short, swift strokes, following the hair's path. I had forgotten to bring a strop, but Hector never allowed his body hair to grow for long—he needed the shave as much as a young girl would. This was an exhibition, after all. The blade stayed keen and I moved up his legs, careful and patient with the knee's tricky angles. I longed to ask him how he had created this body but that wasn't my role here; I had a nonspeaking part. I ran the razor along the muscled slope of his thighs, listening to the hushed rasp of steel over skin, and blessed the man who decided he could not make this party.

I shaved him from the sharp V of his pelvic girdle to the skin around his nut-brown nipples, from the flat hard wall of his belly to the vaulted arches of his armpits. I wished someone would strap tumescence-sensors to the cocks of all the men at the Republican National Convention, then let Hector strut naked to the stage. The Grand Old Partiers would have gouged their eyes out with their thumbs—Hector was irresistible.

"Turn him around!" yelled the photographer. "We don't want to see his *face* all day. Come on, show us his better side."

I gripped his pelvis lightly and he followed my direction, faintly smiling, turning about-face. One of the twelve spectators moaned loudly. Another murmured "Amen to that," and they all laughed. I scrubbed Hector's haughty backside with soapy water and he thrust against me, flirting with his hips.

"The real question," said the critic, "is who the hell goes second?"

Hector arced his back and stared at me over his shoulder, forever half-smiling. There is a certain meanness to the coquette, the cat's cruelty, playing a game with a creature helplessly in its power. But even his cruelty thrilled me.

At last I was ready for his face. I pressed my chest against his, wrapping an arm around his waist to keep him still. Not that he needed to be kept still: Hector could hold a pose for hours. But I wanted my free hand down there, caressing his still slick hips. I shaved his throat, tilting his chin back with the thumb of my blade hand to keep his skin taut, shaved his jawline, shaved the hollow below his cheekbones. When I was finished I ran my palms over his face and body, checking for missed stubble. Finally I closed the razor and stepped back from my work. From the tarsal bones of his ankles to the edges of his long sideburns, Hector was immaculately hairless.

Hector spun on one foot, the other tucked against his thigh. The turn complete he stood on his right leg, bent forward from the hip, extended his right arm to the front and his left leg and arm to the back, parallel to the floor—an angle-perfect arabesque. I realized that Hector was a dancer, that such a fact should have been obvious to me: these were dancer's legs, elegant yet brutally powerful, dancer's arms, sculpted from years of lifting ballerinas, graceful from endlessly practicing the port de bras.

When I first moved to the city, one of my new friends told me never to date a dancer. "They're bitchy little queens," he said. "The lot of them. You fall in love with their perfect asses and they shit all over you."

The spectators applauded and Hector gave a deep bow, then took my hand and we bowed together.

The party kept going until early morning, the other men partnering up and shaving each other. Water fights, mock wrestling, ass slapping—the usual locker-room antics. But the electricity was gone. Nobody else had a straightedge. Nobody else had Hector. Every man in that room wanted to fuck him, but he sat with me, on satin-slipped pillows piled in a dim corner of the room. We spoke in low tones and the other men stared at us. The art critic seemed particularly amused; at one point he called over to us: "Beware, young men. Dancers and painters make ill-fated couples. Think of Isadora Duncan."

We did not think of Isadora Duncan. We talked for hours,

every now and then walking out to the living room to fetch new drinks and stare at the rainy city. I felt a little stupid ordering vodka from a pale girl while sporting a semi-erection, but she never looked at me, only stole quick glances at Hector when he was facing the other way.

"Come see me dance," he ordered me, sipping from a glass of mineral water.

"I'd love to."

"We open this weekend. *Rite of Spring.* Do you like Stravinsky? It's a very difficult dance, very harsh, very hard for the dancer."

"Good luck with it."

Hector widened his eyes in mock horror. "No, no. Never say *good luck* to a dancer."

"Break a leg?"

He crossed himself. "God forbid. No, no. Never. Say, merde."

"Merde? Really?"

"Merde."

Hector told me he wanted to move on to acting; he felt that dance was a small world, that it limited him. Being the danseur in his company's biggest productions, Romeo in *Romeo and Juliet*, Prince Desiré in *Sleeping Beauty*, wasn't enough for him. He wanted an audience of millions. He wanted to be in movies.

I listened to him talk and worked it out in my mind. I'd abandon my paints and man the camera; Hector could be the star. I'd zoom in for a close-up and he could smile his famous smile, bright teeth shining for all of America, a wink for the world to swoon by.

Sometime after midnight he beckoned for me to follow him again. He led me down dark corridors and into a vast bedroom. The rumpled sheets of an unmade bed; the paisley pajamas sprawled across a bench by the bed's footboard; the leather-bound photo album splayed open, plastic sleeves filled with photographs of Hector—all blue-lit from the still-blazing city outside the floor-to-ceiling windows. Hector, blue-skinned, placed his palms against the glass and stared at the neighboring buildings.

"Do you think anyone can see us up here?" he asked.

"Maybe," I said. He was silent and I added, "Everyone in this city is a voyeur. Right this second hundreds of telescopes are trained on us."

"I hope so," he said, shimmying his hips and laughing. "Do you like me, Alexander?"

"God, yes."

"Do you want me?"

I said nothing. I ran the backs of my hands up his thighs and began kissing him, everywhere, acres of tawny, silken skin. He set his feet wide apart and leaned into the window, and I thought: *If we should fall forty stories they can pry my smile from the pavement below.*

3

After the shaving party he hired me to paint his portrait. I hadn't done any portraiture since school; the last three years had been spent on my water-tower series, "Water Towers: 1-59," and I doubted that I could do Hector's form justice.

I was right; each study I began was an exercise in reduction. The full Hector wasn't emerging on the paper. He stood naked on the concrete floor of my Red Hook studio, a converted butcher shop that I had leased with Tulip, an on-again, off-again lesbian from Manitoba.

"If she's on-again, off-again," asked Hector, after I had described my living situation, "why doesn't she call herself bisexual?"

"She thinks bisexual is a cop-out."

Hector raised his eyebrows. "But fucking men is not?"

"Shut up and pose."

"She should only fuck gay men," he said, hands behind his back, smiling coyly to flash his dimples. "If she's worried about the politics."

I looked up from my sketchpad. "Tulip's not your type," I said, and Hector shrugged.

"You don't sleep with women?" I asked. "Do you?"

"Only when I want to."

I resumed my work. "Don't flex, okay? Just stand still."

He stuck his tongue out at me. "When does Four-Lip come home, anyway?"

"Any second now. Where you're standing, that used to be where the meat grinder was. The first six months after we moved in, the whole place reeked of beef."

"Look at me," he said, staring down at the small state of his cock. "Look at poor little me."

"Are you cold?"

"No," he said, "I'm lonely." I dropped the pad and went to him.

. . .

The hardest part of Hector to capture on canvas was his feet. The rest of him was classically proportioned, the marmoreal angles and curves of Grecian statuary, but his feet were ugly. He had dancer's feet, lumpy with knots and contusions, hammertoed, yellow with thick calluses. But Hector was proud of them; he walked around barefoot even when he was clothed, which was a rarity indoors. His feet helped me to understand him. Hector was a Puerto Rican from the Bronx. For all his flirtatious strutting, for all his preening before the mirror, Hector was a tough guy, as much athlete as artist.

One night we were invited to a costume party in Scarsdale hosted by a magazine editor (Hector was invited; I went along as his guest). I picked him up at his apartment and gasped when he opened the door. He wore a black spandex full-length bodysuit, so tight I could read the veins in his biceps, could see that he wore no underwear.

"You're not actually wearing that," I said. I grew up in a Pennsylvania town once known for steel and now known for birthing NFL linebackers; I always felt there was a fine line between gay pride and suicide.

"Of course I am," he said, kissing me on the mouth. "I'm Catman!"

"Catman? There is no Catman. You mean Catwoman?"

"Fuck Catwoman. Catman!"

There was no getting out of it. I was masquerading as an investment banker: I wore a pin-striped suit with a red tie and red suspenders and would carry a five-foot-long penis, but the penis was inflatable, I didn't have to blow it up until we got to the party.

On the subway ride to Grand Central Station I sat on the bench, blushing, while Hector stood above me, refusing to hold on to anything, swaying back and forth to the train's rhythm and humming the same three bars of Prokofiev over and over. Behind him sat a row of elderly women gripping shopping bags. They never took their eyes off him. I had an idle fantasy that they might spring from their seats as one and devour him with gummy jaws.

In the great room of Grand Central, beneath the painted constellations, Hector actually cartwheeled—*cartwheeled*— three times in succession and laughed when he saw me biting my lip. He waved to a frowning cop who stood by the information kiosk, twirling his billy club.

"Come on," I said to Hector, pushing him forward. "It leaves in two minutes."

"The problem with spandex," said Hector, pinching the fabric between his legs, "is it chafes."

We boarded our train and chose an empty car. Hector sighed, frustrated at being cooped-up for forty minutes. A band of high school kids wearing their varsity jackets ran hooting into our car just before the train pulled away. The sight of them, their shaved heads and class rings, triggered warning alarms for me, but Hector seemed not to notice the boys. He rested his head on my shoulder and napped.

The boys noticed us. It started with smirks and whispered jokes. One of them lay his head on his friend's shoulder in imitation of Hector; the friend pushed him away with mock disgust. The ticket collector passed through the car and I bought our tickets. I watched his blue-shirted back disappear through the sliding doors.

They started throwing things at us. First a paper airplane glided over our heads. Then balled-up pages from a newspaper. I nudged Hector with my shoulder; I wanted to move, to get into a car with people. Hector opened his eyes just as a crumpled soda can flew into my lap. He grabbed the can, sat up, and hurled it at the largest kid in the pack, a blue-eyed beefy bruiser. The can hit the boy on the nose and ricocheted away. Before the boy could decide what to do, Hector stood and leaned forward, thick forearms draped over the seat in front of him.

"When was the last time you got your face broke by a man in a catsuit?"

The boy had no answer. At the next stop a large family stepped into our car, broke the silence with the blessed cries of toddlers, and we made it to Scarsdale without further event.

"We're taking a cab back," I told Hector as we walked out of the station. "I'll pay."

"You'd better pay," he said. "You think I've got room for a wallet?"

4

As we walked out one evening, walking through Chinatown, dodging the swarms of rushing people, pointing at the hanging ducks, the suckling pigs spitted and roasted, the crabs peering out from their glass tanks, their pincers clamped in blue rubber bands, Hector opened his mouth to say something but coughed instead, and kept coughing; he stood in the middle of the sidewalk with his hands on his knees, his body convulsed by fits of dry coughs. I held his shoulders for a full minute as pedestrians veered wide of us, none of them slowing for an instant.

"I've got to get out of this city," he told me when he could finally speak, his eyes red. "I swear to God I'm allergic to New Yorkers."

It was a brave joke. We had our blood tested and we heard the diagnosis pronounced. So we learned a new language. We read every article we could find on the new treatments. I called friends I hadn't spoken to in years, sick friends who had quietly retreated from the desperate rounds of parties, dance clubs, and openings. I had dropped these men from my daily thoughts and it shamed me, it shamed me that I listened for signs of gratification in their voices when I told them the news.

Some of them snapped at me, berated me for never visiting, and I accepted their anger for what it was. When the gardener yells at you for trampling his grass, it's not just you he's yelling at. It's every shortcutting bastard for the past ten years, every shirtless boy stomping through the azaleas, every yellow Labrador clawing up the newly planted turf. You are the last in a line of trespassers, and you bear the blame for every offender that has passed this way before.

I quizzed all my infected friends, asked them for names of good doctors and hospitals. I listened to them speak, took notes, and realized how grateful they were for the chance to unleash their tongues. They raged against the government, against their insurance carriers, against the men who infected them and the lovers who left them, against the pretty boys who would not meet their eyes, against a country that wanted them to die and get it over with.

I won't get like that, I told myself. I'd rather put a bullet through my mouth than end as a bundle of hatred and fear. Not all of the men, though, had slipped into this loop of re-criminations. Some were more hopeful. They spoke with great intensity about experimental new medicines, powerful drugs that were rumored to work. Nothing had been feder-ally approved yet; only test subjects had access to the drugs.

Hector nodded when I told him this news. He already knew, had already called his powerful friends ("Patrons of the arts," he told me, winking) and arranged for both of us to meet with a renowned doctor currently conducting tests at a midtown hospital.

"What we're doing," Dr. Kislyany told us, sitting behind neat stacks of papers and journals on his dust-free desk, "is trying to sterilize the bad guys. When we talk about a viral load, you know what that refers to?"

"I think so," I said. Hector rolled his eyes at me. "But not really," I added.

Dr. Kislyany smiled. He was a surprisingly young man, dark and trim and elegant. He wore wire-frame glasses; del-icate butterflies winged across the yellow field of his tie. "The virus clones itself, essentially. It replicates, makes copies. The number of copies floating through a milliliter of blood, that's the viral load. Now, the therapy we're studying here, you understand it was just born? This is an entirely new class of drug. We don't know yet what the long-term ef-fects might be. And we don't know if the drugs work. Early results look pretty promising, but it's too early to tell. It's risky, is what I'm saying. If you decide to do this, if you volunteer, you're making yourselves human guinea pigs."

Hector was staring out the window. I looked at him and then at the doctor. "If it was you," I asked him, "if you were sitting over here, is this the best way to go?"

"I'm pretty sure it's the only way to go."

He handed us long contracts that released the hospital, the drug companies, and everyone else in the world from liability. We read the clauses quickly and signed our names, asking no questions.

"Now we check your blood. If the viral load's below five thousand, we hold off. If it's above, we begin. And gentlemen," he told us, removing his glasses, "this is aggressive therapy. It's not take a couple aspirin, call me in the morning. These pills, they're heavyweights."

We nodded, impatient to begin. I could feel the virus spreading through my body, spawning one hundred offspring a second, each of them intent on rotting me from the inside.

A nurse wearing long rubber gloves and a facemask drew our blood. The next morning Dr. Kislyany called us. Hector's count was eighteen thousand; mine was twenty-five thousand. When we walked out of the hospital, into the cold winter sunshine, Hector asked me to move in with him.

"I want you around," he said. "I'll never remember what to take when. And you're a better cook than me." Being a better cook than Hector was no great compliment; all he ate were protein shakes and raw vegetables. But he didn't want me to putter around the stove; he wanted me to watch over him. As long as I was there to bear witness, Hector could not disappear.

So I moved in with him, leaving Tulip and the butcher shop and Red Hook for Hector and his two-bedroom apartment in TriBeCa. It was my first time living in Manhattan. I had always imagined that when I finally made it to the city I would have *arrived*, with a one-man show in a Soho gallery and a slobbering review in *Art Forum*. But Hector was the one with the scrapbook of magazine reviews, with newspaper photographs of himself onstage, with a bundle of fan mail from actual fans (though mostly, he admitted to me, from his mother).

We began the first of many drug cycles. "Cocktail hour," Hector would say, arranging the amber vials of pills on his kitchen table into separate stacks: *Hector's Morning; Alexander's Morning. Hector's Evening; Alexander's Evening.*

In those first days of living together we saw the pills as our little heroes, fresh-scrubbed American soldiers marching through Paris, waving to the cheering crowds. Nucleoside analogs, nonnucleoside reverse transcriptase inhibitors, protease inhibitors—we pronounced the names reverently, adoringly. They had come to save our lives.

Our affection for the pills did not last long. We had to plan our days around our medication, to remember that didanosine must be taken on an empty stomach, saquinavir with a high-fat meal, indinavir with a low-fat meal; that ritonavir tastes like acid and ought to be drunk with chocolate milk; that delavirdine must be mixed with eight ounces of water and swallowed rapidly, like a frat-boy chugging his beer. I learned that amivudine causes headaches, insomnia, and fatigue; that nevirapine triggers vomiting, diarrhea, fever, and violent purple blooms on the skin—the same symptoms as nelfinavir, except when nelfinavir is taken with saquinavir you feel that knives are carving through your ribs. Zalcitabine ate a hole in the lining of my esophagus. "Minor ulcer," Dr. Kislyany told me, staring at a sonogram of my throat. "Painful, not dangerous." Idovudine inhibits the production of new bone marrow, which meant nothing to me until I contracted pernicious anemia and lost forty pounds and the color from my skin, lost so much strength that for two weeks I could only walk with the aid of a cane. Every time I stood too quickly a swarm of bright flies flashed across my eyes. Painful and dangerous, but I recovered.

The first accident happened nine months into therapy, standing on a street corner, waiting for the light to change. I felt a tremor in my bowels and then the terrible wetness running down my thighs. My mind flashed an image of my four-year-old self, bawling on the overgrown lawn as my mother hollered at me. The light changed and I crossed the street.

Shame is black shit seeping into your pants' legs, into your socks, as you climb the backstairs of your lover's apartment building. Shame is bundling your dirtied clothes in a garbage bag and dropping them down the incinerator chute. Shame is standing in the shower, the water as hot as you can bear, scouring your skin with pumice, rubbing the skin raw, until stars of blood constellate the legs, and harder still, wanting to flay yourself, to step out of this hide, to slither free of this spoiled body.

Kislyany prescribed antidiarrheal pills and they worked too well; I could not move my bowels for six days. I stopped taking the antidiarrheals. Two months later I had another accident. I began wearing adult diapers. Kislyany gave me different pills, ones that allowed me to resume a natural rhythm, and after a few months I felt safe walking the streets without a diaper.

Hector remained unfazed by each new cycle of medication. I would lie in the darkened bedroom, counting to a thousand and promising myself that when I reached that number the migraine would disappear, while through the door I heard the television set and Hector's quiet laughter. He was unaffected by the nausea that plagued me. When I knelt before the toilet's open mouth, the ceramic bowl splattered with orange vomit, Hector would wipe my lips with a wet towel and squeeze the back of my neck. I would spit in the bowl and look up at him, at Hector as beautiful as ever, at Hector watching himself nurse me in the bathroom mirror.

A strange thing happened. Every three months we had our viral load checked, and despite the adverse reactions I began responding to the therapy. My count shrank to five thousand and hovered in that vicinity. The virus wasn't going anywhere for a while, but it wasn't able to replicate either. My body and the disease were engaged in a stalemate. But Hector's count increased, from eighteen thousand to twenty-four, twenty-four to forty, forty to fifty-two, fifty-two to fifty-four, fifty-four to ninety. He was still dancing, his body remained muscular and lithe, but the monsters were breeding.

Eighteen months after I moved in, on a bright June Sunday, he called for me. I ran into the bathroom, saw him standing before the mirror, his mouth open. His tongue was coated with a milky film. Thrush.

I called Kislyany at his home in Westchester. I could hear the screams of young children in the background, and the whine of a blender, and below everything Bach's great fugue for organ. I told him what had happened.

"All right," he said, and I thought, *Please don't use that phrase, Doctor.* "It's been heading this way for a while. How are *you* feeling?"

"Me? Listen, should I bring him into the hospital?"

"How's his breathing?"

"His breathing's okay. Is this— Does thrush mean for sure?"

"Put that down, Julia," he said. "Thank you, sweetheart. Sorry, Alexander. Say again?"

"Does thrush mean for sure?"

He sighed into the telephone and I could picture him removing his wire-frame glasses, rubbing his tired eyes with the back of his hand. "I could tell you nothing's certain until we do tests. But yes, it's for sure. He has AIDS. Bring him into the hospital tomorrow morning, we'll give him some antifungal for the thrush. It clears up quickly."

"Tomorrow morning?"

"Unless you want to go to the emergency room. Come in tomorrow, we'll X-ray his chest, see if anything's in there."

The next morning rubber-gloved, face-masked doctors and nurses subjected Hector to a battery of tests. A serpentine tube, a bronchoscope, was twisted down into his windpipe, where it scraped a small tissue sample for microscopic examination. They laid him down naked on a steel mechanized table and covered his groin with a lead pad, then X-rayed various parts of his body. Three different nurses jabbed three different needles into his arm for three different blood tests.

Afterward we sat next to each other in Kislyany's office. I tried to hold Hector's hand but he wouldn't let me; he stared out the window at the buildings across the way.

"You have to stay here tonight, Hector," Kislyany said. "You'll have to stay for a while. You've got pneumonia."

Hector slowly turned his head to look at the doctor. "Pneumonia?"

"Parasitic pneumonia. *Pneumocystis carinii.* We'll get you on pentamidine for that, but I need to keep you here. It's— It boggles the mind that you're able to move around so well. Most cases the patient can't walk across a room without help. That's a good sign. Here's a bad sign: Your T-four lymphocytes are at one-twenty. That's low; that's getting way too low. We're going to switch over to a new series of meds—"

"Who's we? You and me?"

"No—"

"Alexander and me?"

"Figure of speech," said Kislyany. "Alexander's pills are working; he'll stick with those. For you it's antibiotics for the pneumonia, antifungals for the thrush, whole new regimen. I've got a room reserved for you on the eighth floor, nice room, sunlight."

. . .

Hector fought off the pneumonia in three days, to Kislyany's astonishment. The hospital released him and Hector returned to his rehearsals, weakened but eager to dance. He slowly gained his strength back. In August he was reinstated as danseur, a noble but doomed gesture on the company's part. A few weeks after that, limbering up at the studio, Hector's heel slipped off the barre and he crashed to his back. Three ballerinas came to our apartment that night; they teased Hector for his clumsiness and we all laughed, but I saw that the ballerinas were frightened. Hector never fell.

The following Monday I came home with a bag of groceries and found Hector sitting at the kitchen table, staring at his hands.

"Rehearsal canceled?" I asked him, putting the milk in the refrigerator.

"I'm taking a leave," he said, his eyes dry and dark and unknowable.

. . .

It made no sense to me that Hector's body was quitting, that my own kept battling and holding its own. It seemed stupid to me. It seemed criminal.

Things got worse. I would find him standing in the living room and ask him what he was looking for. He would stare at me blankly and then blink, half-smile, and shrug. Once, while I was painting in the guest bedroom, I heard a thud from the bathroom. I ran in there and found him kneeling naked in the shower, the water beating down on him, a red bruise already darkening his forehead.

"What happened? Are you okay?"

He picked a tangle of my hair out of the drain and held it up to me. "You're going bald, Alexander," he told me sadly.

When he watched the television sitcoms he no longer laughed; he stared at the TV as if he were waiting for someone to step through the glass. When I turned the power off he did not seem to notice; he'd continue to gaze at the empty screen for minutes.

I woke up on a rainy October morning to a strange moaning; turning over in bed I saw Hector lying facedown, his right arm twitching. I thought he was having a nightmare and poked him in the side. He did not wake up. I rolled him onto his back and saw that his eyes were open, twin trails of drool leaked from the corners of his mouth.

I called for an ambulance and the paramedics came, lifted him off the bed, strapped him into a stretcher, and drove us to the hospital. Dr. Kislyany met me in the waiting room, a manila folder in his hand, a pencil behind his ear. He led me to his office and closed the door.

"It's bad, Alexander." He pulled a sheaf of transparencies from the folder. "He has lymphoma of the brain. We ran a few CAT scans."

I looked down at the black-and-white images of Hector's brain. Kislyany indicated a white blur with the eraser of his pencil. "See that mass?" He indicated another one. "That one? They're all over. Lesions." He exhaled loudly and tapped his desktop with the pencil.

"What do we do?" I asked. The pencil-taps sounded loud as bombs.

"We'll start radiation treatment tomorrow. I've reserved the same room for him, the one on the eighth floor. Listen, Alexander, how are *you* feeling?"

I did not understand what he wanted.

"Your viral count was very low last time," he said, nodding approvingly. "Under four thousand. We're headed in the right direction."

. . .

The next day hospital technicians began blasting Hector's head with X-rays. As the weeks went by his body started to wither, the muscle melting from his bones, the bones surging against his skin, the skin sagging and fading until it seemed no more than cheap paper hastily wrapped around last-minute gifts.

For two weeks in November he seemed to improve. He would lie awake for a few hours at a time, and nod at me as I spoon-fed him custard and applesauce, and half-smile as I wiped his lips clean.

On one of those occasions he asked me to bring his portrait into the hospital.

"I never finished it," I told him. "It never looked as good as you."

"Bring it," he said. "I want to see it."

The next day I brought him the painting, the frame sandwiched between two sheets of corrugated cardboard. I had painted Hector nude and didn't want people on the street, in the subway, to stare at his unclothed image. Hector nodded when I showed him the painting, and directed me to rest it on the windowsill.

"You want everyone to see it?" I asked, looking at the painting. The muscular, healthy Hector stared back at me. But that was a stupid question. I placed the painting on the windowsill and stepped back.

"No," he said, closing his eyes. "I don't like the frame. Not black. Get something in wood, a pale wood."

Later in the week, when the painting was newly framed, he nodded. "That's nice. I look good."

"You do," I told him. "You look good."

"What's not finished?"

"Your feet," I said. I pointed at his painted legs that ended at the ankles. In the painting Hector floated, nothing but space between the butcher shop's concrete floor and where he began.

Hector smiled and closed his eyes. "Feet are hard."

. . .

On New Year's Eve I smuggled a bottle of champagne into Hector's eighth-floor room. He had lost consciousness a week before. I filled plastic cups for both of us, sat beside him and watched the television, watched the ball drop, watched thousands of small bulbs light the giant number *1994*, watched fireworks explode on the small screen. A nurse came into the room to check his breathing and pulse; she wagged her finger at me but then accepted a drink. She stayed with us for ten minutes and joined me in a chorus of "Auld Lang Syne."

"Happy New Year," she said as she was leaving the room. "I'll be back in two hours."

When she left I pulled my chair close to Hector's bed and leaned forward to kiss his forehead. His skin was hot and damp. I was used to that; the fever had come and gone for months. His body was collapsing upon itself. If I placed my palm against his chest-bone and pushed, he would crumble like ash. His yellow face rested on a white pillowcase, his lips dry and blue, partly open. A patchy stretch of beard grew along his jaw. His lower lip bulged like a ballplayer's with a wad of chewing tobacco; I pulled the lip from his teeth and saw the wine-grapes of Kaposi's sarcoma jutting from his gums.

I stood wearily from the bed and walked into the bathroom, turned on the hot water, and waited until it steamed from the faucet. I wet a hand towel, lathered it with liquid soap, returned to Hector, and daubed his face gently with the cotton cloth. I drew the tortoiseshell handle from my pocket and opened the blade. While fireworks continued to flare on the television, I shaved the coarse whiskers from Hector's face. After I was done, after I had sponged off the soapy residue and patted his face dry with a clean towel, I stood above him with the razor open in my hand. I thought how easy it would be to cut his throat, how good it would be for him, something in the way of mercy. But I could never do it; I could never raise my hand against Hector, not even for mercy.

That night I understood the old story for the first time, that the wooden horse is Love, allowed through the gates against all warnings, bearing its cargo of killers, men with long knives who crawl from the dark belly and burn the city down.

One week later he was dead and buried with the winter dead.

. . .

The new antiviral therapy, of course, was hailed as a great success. Beaming doctors graced the covers of magazines, test tubes in hand, beneath jubilant banners: *Hope for the Hopeless, The Virus Hunters, Man of the Year, A Cure at Last?* I read story after story lauding the scientists' ingenuity, their exhaustive research and testing, how they sprang back from each defeat to renew the attack.

I looked at diagrams of the drugs' molecular composition; I read the dates of FDA approval. I scanned charts that listed percentile scores for the drugs: their efficacy in lowering the viral count or raising the T4 count, their rates of specific toxicities. The numbers were ordered in two parallel columns, statistics for people given the drugs lined up against statistics for people given placebos. I read that nevirapine caused nausea in forty-seven percent of the patients, against three percent for the placebo group. Breathing hard, I read two years of drug-induced symptoms in a single row of italics, side-effects I had suffered and many more I had escaped: kidney stones, bilirubin, abdominal pain, fatigue, flank pain, diarrhea, vomiting, acid regurgitation, loss of appetite, dry mouth, back pain, headache, insomnia, dizziness, taste changes, rash, respiratory infection, anemia, peripheral neuropathy, hepatoxicity, pancreatitis, ulcers, dry skin, sore throat, fever, indigestion, muscle pain, anxiety, depression, itching, painful irritation, gallbladder inflammation, cirrhosis of the liver. I believed I could hear a rhyme-scheme in the procession of words, a rhythm, and I thought: *These words mean nothing to whoever typed them, they are mere collections of letters, unburdened of pain.* I thought: *These are the miseries of the lucky, of the survivors.* I read the percentiles for the placebo-users: two percent, two percent, zero percent, one percent—and something made sense. I dropped the journal to the floor and shut my eyes.

The next morning I banged on Kislyany's office door. A nurse, carrying a clipboard in one hand and a cup of coffee in the other, walked by and smiled.

"How you feeling, Alexander?"

I banged on the door again and Kislyany opened it. Two young men sat by his desk, one black, one white, their heads bowed together, speaking in low, urgent tones. They held contracts in their hands.

"Alexander," said Kislyany. "What's the matter? Are you feeling all right?"

He was one of the heroes of the great medical victory, and success had treated him well. He leaned against the door frame, handsome and urbane, one hand in the pocket of his gray wool cardigan. His initial expression was of warmth and concern. The look on my face changed his mind; he raised his palms to me before I said a word.

"You let him die," I said. "You knew what was happening and you let him die."

I didn't think I was speaking loudly, but the two young men turned to stare at me. Kislyany stepped out of his office and nodded to them.

"Give me a minute, gentlemen." He closed the door behind him.

"He never got real pills, did he?"

"Why don't we take a walk, Alexander." Kislyany tried to rest his hand on my elbow but I pushed it off. "Alexander—"

"Did he?"

"No. He was part of the control group." Kislyany saw the way my face twisted and he quickly added, "This is the way medical research works. It has to be this way."

"You let him die. You were his doctor for his two years and you gave him nothing but sugar pills. You let him die."

He grabbed me by the shoulders and pulled me close, his eyes narrow and angry. "You think I work this hard because I want people to die? Listen to me. We didn't know if the pills would work when we started. Nobody knew. This is brand-new research; for all we knew the pills would kill more people than the virus. Okay? It has to be done this way. The drugs have to be tested. There always has to be a control group."

The phrase *control group* hung there in the fluorescent light, cold, precise, and merciless.

"But why did he have to be in it? He would still be here, Doctor. Why did you pick me? Who told you to pick me?"

He released my collar and shook his head. "I didn't pick you. It's all random. A computer selects the names randomly. It was just luck, Alexander."

My legs felt boneless below me; I feared I would collapse onto the linoleum floor. I didn't want to be weak now; I prayed for strength.

"He would've beaten it," I said quietly. "If you gave him the drugs, he would've beaten it."

"It was double-blind. He didn't know, I didn't know.

That's the way all tests are conducted. It's the way it has to work. I'm not the bad guy, Alexander. I know you want a bad guy, but there is none. Not me, not the FDA, nobody. This is my life, this *is it*, trying to find a cure for this goddamn disease. Two years ago we didn't know if the pills worked. Now we know. Those men in there," he said, nodding toward the closed door, "they have a chance to live long lives."

I rested my face against the beige wall, my cheek flush with the cold paint. I could hear the gurgle of water running through pipes, and hammering from somewhere below us; I imagined I could feel the flow of electricity running through copper wires.

"I don't want a bad guy, Doctor. I want Hector."

He nodded. "I'm sorry, Alexander. I saw him dance once. *Sleeping Beauty*. I know nothing about ballet but—" He shrugged and smiled. "He had the whole audience in the palm of his hand. Listen, we've probably got these two guys in here panicked. Let me finish up with them and we'll go get something to eat." He gripped my arm for a moment and then reached for the doorknob.

"Doctor," I said, and he paused there, waiting. "You knew. You knew my pills were working, you knew for a long time. Don't say anything for a second, okay? Please, don't say anything. When you saw what was happening, you could have given him the real drugs. Maybe it would have been too late, I don't know. But you could have tried. Hector could have—"

Kislyany's face closed down on me. He entered his office

and shut the door behind him. In that moment, while the door was still partway open, I saw the two young lovers sitting a few feet apart, holding hands across the gap. One of them looked right at me, his eyes fearful and curious. The other stared out the window.

5

The stewardess returns with the co-pilot, a broad-jawed man, his sleeves rolled to the elbows. He scowls as he comes close and waves at the air with his hand.

"How long has he been sitting like this?" he asks the stewardess, his voice low but angry.

"Maybe fifteen minutes. I think he's sick, Jimmy."

"You think he's sick? No kidding he's sick." The co-pilot bends toward me, until his face is inches from mine. "Look at me, buddy," he whispers. He wrinkles his nose. "Look at me."

I look at him. We stare at each other for several seconds.

"Last chance," he says. "Come with us or we're carrying you back there."

He waits for me to answer. When he sees that I won't, he reaches forward to unbuckle my belt. I don't interfere; this has gone on long enough. I don't want to be here anymore, among these people.

The co-pilot signals the steward and then kneels down to grab my ankles. The steward holds me by the armpits and together they hoist me from my seat, grunting as they go. Most of the passengers are standing now. They watch in silence, already rehearsing the stories they will tell when they're back on the ground, about the madman on their flight.

I go limp in the crewmen's arms and let them carry me to the rear of the plane. They shove me into the lavatory. "I'm standing right here," the steward says before closing the door. "You're not going anywhere until we land."

Here at last I strip off my soiled clothes. I wet paper towel after paper towel and sponge the filth from my body. I pump liquid soap into my hands and clean myself as best I can.

There were days when I wanted to see Kislyany's daughter bleeding from the eyes. I wanted him to come to me, desperate and weeping, begging for help. I would hand him sugar cubes and say, "Feed her these. She's part of the control group. This is the way it works."

I'm past that now. I wish the girl a long life and happiness. But I want her to know that the grass she walks on is lush with the rot of beautiful men. *And as to you Corpse I think you are good manure.* What grows from the dung is what feeds us; we graze upon the graves. I want Kislyany's daughter to know that. I want the country to know that.

If I had to do it all over again, I would have made it work. Hector would be a movie star and I would film his every move, twenty-four framed Hectors per second. Twenty-four still-lifes. He would shimmer on screens everywhere, and then to video, Hector in every family's living room. He'd play Prince Desiré on sets across the nation; kiss Aurora and wake her from the hundred-year slumber, rewind and wake her again, rewind and wake her again.

I sit naked on the closed toilet seat and fall asleep to the engine's steady hum. We fly west, thirty thousand feet above nighttime America.

ACKNOWLEDGMENTS

Sherwin B. Nuland's beautiful book, *How We Die: Reflections on Life's Final Chapter,* was a great help in the writing of "Merde for Luck." I thank my wonderful teachers: Ernest Hebert, Geoffrey Wolff, and Michelle Latiolais. Thank you, Molly Stern; I wish you could edit the rest of my life. Thanks also to my fellow students at U.C. Irvine, to my agents Owen Laster, Alicia Gordon, and Jennifer Ragains-Riggio, and to D. B. Weiss, whose wise counsel and late-night emails saved me from writing even worse sentences than the ones you've already read.